Dedication

I wish to dedicate this book my book to my sister, Kathy, whose selfless words and thoughtful actions often serve to keep our late mother's memory fresh in my mind and heart.

I love you, sis!

Nightfall Over Nicodemus

by
RG Yoho

CHAPTER ONE

Every time the horse would move or switch his tail, the noose would pull tighter around the broad-shouldered, black man's neck.

Sitting astride his horse with his hands tied behind his back, the black man felt the sweat dripping from every pore on his body.

A slap on the rump, the report of a gun, or any loud or unexpected noise would cause the horse to bolt, leaving the man to die a brutal death, suspended between heaven and earth.

Damon Gates softly cursed his bad luck. He remembered his dear wife, sainted mother, and precious son. He wondered how they would ever survive without him.

"I'm telling you, I didn't rustle them cows," Gates said, a statement which was as close to begging for his life as Damon's pride would allow him to go. "I can prove them beeves are mine."

"I know you didn't take them. You ain't hanging for that, buck. The boys and me are fixing to stretch your neck because you're a darkie. Probably a runaway, too."

The pair of men with him laughed at the remark.

Damon didn't respond. They might take his life, but he wouldn't allow anybody to steal his dignity.

Ben spat a green stream of tobacco juice through the place in his mouth where a snaggled tooth once grew. His evil, green eyes danced with excitement at the thought of this former slave, jerking at the end of a rope.

"You have any last words, boy?" the man said, while standing at the flank of Gates' mount.

"Go to hell!" Gates replied.

"My, aren't you a salty one, boy! You talk tough for a man with a noose around his neck."

A veteran of the War Between the States, Ben Anders was still bitter about the surrender of General Robert E. Lee. He blamed the general. He cursed the name of Jeff Davis. He despised Abraham Lincoln. He blamed the Confederacy.

Generally, he was just angry with everyone.

Although the murder of this former slave wouldn't make up for the South losing the war, it didn't really matter. The empty place in Anders' soul only found pleasure in the suffering of others.

"Let's get it over with, Ben."

"What's your hurry, Jeff?" Ben said, making no effort to hide his pleasure. "Look at the man's face. Bet he's wishing he was back on the plantation now."

"Jeff's right, Ben," Wade said, still mounted on horseback. "What if someone sees us here?"

"Little late for that," Jeff added. "Here comes a rider."

The rider was an unshaven, dumpy spectacle on horseback. Nothing about his manner or bearing struck fear in the hearts of any who saw him. The three men laughed at the image of the stranger as he rode up to them.

The rider finally drew rein with his horse, nose-to-nose, in front of the animal Gates was astride.

"I see you boys finally caught one of those darkies. Good for you. Way too many of them running around loose."

After first thinking the man might actually try to break up the lynching, Gates' heart sank at the stranger's comment.

"What's your name, friend?" Anders asked.

"They call me Gabriel Burns."

"I heard of a man by that name down in Texas a few years back," Wade observed. "Supposed to be pretty good with gun work."

"Reckon that would be me," Burns said.

* * * *

THE TEN YEAR OLD, YOUNGSTER INTERRUPTED HIS chores long enough to watch the pair of riders approaching.

Matt Coleman wasn't used to visitors coming to the ranch. Like any child, he longed to know what was happening in town, away from the restricted world of his life there on his father's place.

"Hi there, boy," Walt Jenkins said. He reached inside his saddle bag and removed a peppermint stick, which he gently tossed to the youngster. "There you go."

The boy caught the unexpected treat, smiling as he did so. "Thank you, mister," he said, before plunging it into his mouth.

"Is your pa or ma here?"

"Pa's out buying supplies, but Mama's in the house. Mamaw's there with her."

Jenkins tipped his hat and smiled. "Thank you, son. But you better get back to work now. Wouldn't want your pa to get back and find those chores undone."

"Thanks again, mister!"

As the two riders moved toward the house, Jamie McGregor glared at the ranch foreman. "What's the point in being nice to the boy?" McGregor asked.

"The boy didn't do nothing,"

"Doesn't matter what he did or didn't do. Being nice to the boy's like feeding a stray cat," Jamie observed "His parents have to clear off this land. And when they do, the boy has to go, too."

"Still no call for us to be mean to him."

"Just don't forget where your loyalties are, Walt."

Generally a good-natured soul, Walt quickly grew tired of Jamie's constant scoldings. "Listen, son. I know who pays my salary and it isn't you! Now, why don't you just let me do my job?"

Just about that time, the door to the meager house opened. An attractive, young lady, adorned in a red apron, came out the door. "What can I do for you, gentlemen?"

The smell of baked apples and cinnamon filled the air.

A smiling Walt Jenkins removed his hat. "Good morning, Mrs. Coleman."

Seeing that the young man failed to remove his hat, Walt stared daggers at him. With a scowl, the young McGregor followed suit.

Walt resumed his easy smile "Your boy out there," he

4

said, nodding towards the barn, "said the mister was away. When do you think he'll return?"

"I expect him home about any time," she said, not caring much for the way the young man leered at her figure. "I thought it might be him, when I first heard your horses ride up to the house."

Along with the smell of fresh apple pie, Jenkins noticed the older woman, peering out the window of the house. Walt was certain he briefly caught the glint of a gun barrel trained on the two of them.

Jenkins made certain that he showed so sudden movement. Figuring the kid riding beside him was unaware of the figure in the window, Walt gently reined his horse to a place where the young McGregor was between him and the window glass.

"Well, we're going to go now," Walt said. "Tell your husband that we'll be back in a couple days. I'm going to need an answer as to what I talked to him about earlier."

"And the time for waiting's long since over," Jamie added.

Jenkins cast a doubtful eye at the kid, figuring that kind of rude talk might only get them killed. He couldn't wait to get away from the house and the crazy, old woman holding a gun on them from the window.

"I'll be sure and tell Kane you stopped by again."

"Thank you very much, ma'am," Walt said, tipping his hat. The ranch foreman reined his horse around, while still keeping himself shielded from the house by the other rider. "Let's go, Jamie."

As the two of them rode away, Walt breathed a sigh of relief. "I'm sure glad to get out of there."

McGregor laughed. "What's the matter, Jenkins? You scared of one tiny woman and a little boy? Her old man wasn't even around. Don't guess I'll ever understand why Pa keeps you around as the ranch foreman. Sounds like you might be a little yellow."

Now it was Walt's turn to laugh. He gently drew rein and cast a backward glance towards the house. Walt pushed the bill of his hat up from his eyes. "Since we're talking about things we don't understand, I reckon it's hard for me to believe any of Robert McGregor's seed ever had any part in making you."

"What do you mean by that?"

"Seed, that's what the bull of the herd has. When he gets together with the cows, it leads to the making of baby cows."

Jamie was furious. "I know that, Walt! And you know that isn't what I'm asking about. What did you mean about me not being related to Pa?"

"I've worked for McGregor for many a year now. Your dad's not only a tough man," Walt said, "but he's a smart one, too. To my way of thinking, if brains were poker cards, you couldn't beat a pair of deuces."

"You can't talk to me like that!"

Walt shook out the reins. "Reckon I just did."

"My pa will have you fired for that."

"I doubt it. Come to think of it, I hope you tell him," Walt said. "I don't think he'll do anything but laugh."

"You'd better hope nothing ever happens to him," the young man fired back, "because I'll..."

"You'll do what? From what I saw today, I think you'll be lucky to see another birthday."

6

"What are you talking about?"

"The old woman with the gun."

"What old woman?"

* * * *

A TALL, LEAN MAN WITH TWIN GUNS STEPPED DOWN from his horse. He removed his hat, wiped his brow with the grimy sleeve at the crook of his elbow, and then returned the hat to his head.

He gently patted the horse on the neck and cast a doubtful glance toward the sky. The lone rider figured there were only about two more hours before nightfall.

He was hungry and exhausted from many hours in the saddle, but there was no time to take care of those two needs now.

Taking a long pull from his canteen, Kellen Malone poured the last of the cool, refreshing liquid into his hat and held it up for his horse to drink. Shaking the canteen from side-to-side, he grimaced. Then he hung the empty canteen on the saddle horn.

Dropping the reins, Kellen Malone studied the faint trail the rider left. Then he knelt down beside the trail.

The tracks were fresh; the rider was close. He examined them once more.

I'll probably take you today, tomorrow at the latest.

* * * *

AFTER WATCHING THE PAIR OF RIDERS FINALLY DISappear into the distance, Ann Coleman went back into the house. Closing the door behind her, Ann saw Kane's aged mother still watching from the window.

"They're gone now, Bea." she said. It was only then that she noticed the rifle her mother-in-law was holding. "What are you doing with that rifle?"

"Pretty sure I could've got the young one," she said. "Now that other rider was pretty cagey, Annibel. The way he moved his horse, got a hunch he might have seen me."

Ann jerked the rifle from the woman's hands. She returned the gun to the cabinet against the back wall. "We don't need any more trouble with the McGregors. What if you'd pulled the trigger by accident?"

Bea Coleman laughed. "I suppose we'd have to clean his guts off the side of the house. One less McGregor, one less problem."

"You don't really mean that!"

"Darn tootin' I do!" she said. Bea Coleman freshened up her cup of coffee, which had now gone cold. "Want some?"

"No, thanks," Ann replied, taking a seat at the table.

The older woman joined her there. She placed a gentle hand on her daughter-in-law's shoulder. "We've talked about this before, Annibel. You know Kane is right about what has to be done."

"I know what he's doing, but there has to be some other way," Ann replied, still clinging to a few scattered threads of her old Quaker upbringing, which she left far behind in Pennsylvania with most of her good china.

"Look at it this way, dear. Both of you like this place. Why should you let anyone make you give it up?"

"I don't plan on us losing it," Ann replied. "I just hope there's some way for us to avoid bloodshed."

* * * *

"Sure a good day for a hanging," Burns said, cutting off a slice of tobacco. He rolled it over in his jaw before saying anything more. "You never did say what you were hanging him for. He steal some cows?"

Anders shook his head.

"Must be a killer then."

Gates spoke proudly. "I never killed nobody."

"He harm somebody's woman or kid?"

"Nothing like that," Jeff said.

Burns pushed the hat brim higher off his face. "Reckon I could appreciate this a mite more if I knew the reason for this man's neck getting stretched."

Anders didn't much like being questioned, about anything. "Does it really matter? Ain't it enough that he's black as Satan?"

"Don't really matter to me, friend. Just wanted to make sure hanging was enough for him."

About that time, Wade reined his horse up to the stranger's left. He patted the animal on the flank. "This here's a pretty fine horse. Don't you think, Ben?"

Anders spoke up. "Come to think of it, that there is a right nice piece of horse flesh. Much too nice an animal for a Texican."

"Glad you boys like him," Burns replied.

The latest rider's appearance only made Jeff more nervous about what they were doing. "Come on, boys. Let's hang this man and be done with it! This spot's getting busier than Richmond at Christmas time."

"Okay! Okay!" Ben said. "Quit your nagging, already.

You sound like my last wife." He looked over at the stranger. "Why don't you move your mount out of the way, Burns, and enjoy the fun with us?"

Wade was still admiring the man's horse. "Better still," he added, "why don't you just climb off of him?"

A man of the gun himself, Gabriel Burns had no doubts about what the men's next play would soon be. He knew his only chance of survival was to kill these men before they killed him.

Although there was nothing impressive in the appearance of the Texas gunman, all those who saw him were often amazed by the sheer speed by which he could get into action.

Burns' right hand flashed for his gun, putting a couple of shells in the shirtfront of Ben Anders, who spun around from the impact and tumbled to the ground. Then the man from Texas turned his gun on Wade, who'd already grabbed iron.

Wade's first shot creased Burns' side, doing no serious damage. Another struck the gunman hard, piercing his left shoulder.

With the start of the shooting, Damon's horse tried to bolt, filling the black man's growing eyes with fear.

It was only the position of Burns' mount, nose-to-nose with Damon's horse, that kept Gates in the saddle. Burns struggled with the reins, doing his best to hold his position, while also fighting against the odds to defend his own life.

Due to the pitching of his own horse, Burns' first shot at Wade missed. Gabriel quickly triggered the gun again, a shot which sent the fallen angels racing away with Wade's evil soul.

By this time, the slowest gun hand of the three unlimbered his gun. What Jeff lacked in speed, he more than made up for in accuracy.

His first shot hit the mounted gunman low and hard.

Burns winced at the searing pain in his stomach and turned his gun to meet the final threat. The slug from his six-gun tore an ugly path through Jeff's throat, leaving only a frothy, garbled, and dying call for his mama, a cry soon followed by grim silence.

Despite the seriousness of his wound, Burns holstered his gun, reached out, and took hold of the reins of Damon's frightened horse. "There, boy," he said, as the animal quickly calmed to his touch.

"Thank you, sir," a frightened Damon Gates said. Those were the only words the grateful black man could seem to muster at the moment.

Burns simply smiled and gave a brief nod.

He then reined his horse around behind Gates. Removing a knife from his sheath, Burns reached toward the ropes that bound the man's wrists.

On the ground beside them, a mortally wounded Ben Anders summoned one final ounce of vengeful strength and weakly lifted his gun.

The bullet tore through Burns' chest, knocking the knife from his hands as he fell from the saddle.

Damon's horse, crazed by this latest act of gunplay, went racing away for the distant hills. The noose tightened around the Gates' neck, leaving him dangling from the tree limb.

Had it not been for the years of hard, back-breaking labor, the force would have snapped his neck immediately. But the man's great strength, which prevented a broken neck, did absolutely nothing to keep him from being strangled by the ever-tightening noose around his throat.

As his body swung violently, side-to-side from the tree limb, Gates kicked and danced at the end of the rope, struggling to catch a breath.

Gates knew he was only moments away from death.

Upon seeing the man's plight, Gabriel struggled to rise. Managing only to roll over on his back, he summoned enough energy to pull his gun once more. However, his dreadful blood loss, combined with his dim and failing vision, caused Burns to fire an errant shot at the swinging length of hemp.

The wounded man's empty gun fell from his weakened hand into the dirt.

CHAPTER TWO

Weary and exhausted from his endless days on horseback, Kellen Malone had just about decided to forget about his pursuit of the man until tomorrow. He was simply riding his horse along, searching out a good place to make camp for the night.

Then he heard the voices.

The sounds of conversation were coming from somewhere off in the distance. And although Malone couldn't make out what they were saying, the voices were growing louder and more insistent.

Hearing the first shots, Malone spurred his horse racing down the trail.

Then the gunfire stopped, soon followed by a single blast from a gun.

At the edge of a distant hill, he could see four men on the ground. Hanging from a tree limb was a black man, kicking and thrashing at the end of a rope.

Cursing softly, Malone knew there was no way his horse could reach the black man in time to save his life.

His mind formulating a plan, Malone yanked the rifle from his scabbard and jumped down from the saddle. Scrambling alongside his horse, he levered a shell into the chamber.

Using his saddle for a bench to steady the rifle, he careful took aim at the rope. For just a split-second, Kell recalled his friend's ideas about the wisdom of breaking up a hanging.

Making some quick allowances for the wind and distance, Malone took a deep breath and let it out slowly. Only then did he ease back on the trigger.

The slug from the rifle covered the vast distance in only a heartbeat.

As the black man was gasping for his final breath, the bullet just grazed the rope. The strong, uncoiled length of new hemp began to fray, twist, and finally snap, dropping the man to the earth in a heap.

Even from that distance, Malone smiled as he saw the man fall and heard him make a painful, but living, grunt.

Kell patted the horse softly and returned the weapon to its case. Then he climbed atop his mount and started down the trail toward the dead and dying bodies.

Unsure of what danger he might actually be riding into, one of Malone's six-guns was in his hand as he approached them.

"Are you okay," Kell asked, climbing down from his mount.

"I am now, thanks to you," Gates said, rubbing the painful rope burns that marked his neck. Then he cast an eye at the wounded Burns. "*And* him."

With his gun still drawn, Malone moved from one body

to another, checking them for any remaining signs of life. Seeing that Anders was still scarcely breathing, Kell would take no chances. He kicked away the gun from the dying man's hand.

"That's the one that wanted to hang me," Gates said, "just because he didn't like my skin color."

Kell nodded.

Gates raised his eyebrows, pointing at the fallen body of Gabriel Burns. "That one tried to save my life."

Seeing that Anders could do them no further harm, Kell ignored him. Then he rushed over to the wounded Texas gunman. After discovering Burns still had some signs of life, Gain cast one more cautious glance at Anders before rushing to one of the other horses for a canteen.

Tossing the canteen to Gates, Malone knelt by the man and lifted his head. The black man poured some of the cool water onto his dying lips. Then he held it close, as Burns took a couple more swallows. He winced at the pain.

"Thanks," Gates said, "for what you tried to do for me, Mr. Burns."

"First decent thing I ever done in my life and it got me killed." Then he smiled. "Bet I won't let it happen again." He turned his glance from Gates to Malone. "And just who are you?"

"I'm the guy who's been trailing you for the past two weeks."

"Congratulations, mister!" he said with a grin. "Looks like you finally got me. Sorry I ain't got no prizes for you." Then his face turned serious. "What in the world did I ever do that would make a man I never laid eyes on chase me for two whole weeks?"

"You murdered one of my ranch hands in Arizona, just outside a saloon called the Lucky Lady."

Burns' eyes went wide. "Yea, now I remember that place. Big, husky bartender there."

"His name's Halstead. Buck Halstead."

"Yea, that's right," Burns said." Some of the biggest hands I ever saw on a man."

"Tommy, the boy you killed, he was only a kid."

"But his gun was full-grown, mister." Burns coughed suddenly, reaching over to hold his chest from the pain it caused him. "And the boy couldn't hold his whiskey. Darn fool tried to brace me."

"I didn't know that."

"Might of talked him out of it, but I didn't much care at the time."

Gates offered the Texan another drink, which he refused. Still holding the canteen, he started over to the outlaw. One quick look told him that the soul of Ben Anders had already moved on to its place of lasting darkness.

"Sorry about the circumstances, but I'm happy to finally meet a boss who will fight for one of those working for him." Burns managed another pained smile. "If I'd had a couple bosses like you, it might have led me down a brighter path."

"Mr. Burns, you shouldn't talk now," Gates offered.

"It don't much matter," Burns said. "They'll be plenty of time for resting soon."

"Anything I can do for you?" Gates asked

"Don't have no family anymore. And news of my death would just bring too much joy to the woman who once wore my ring." The man's voice was growing more difficult to hear. "Couple things you *can* do for me, though."

"What are they?"

"Don't let the buzzards get me."

Kell spoke up. "I'll see that you get a decent burial."

"What's the other one?" Asked Gates.

"After I'm gone, there's a letter in my pocket. It has some money in it, money they paid me to help them."

"Okay."

"Make sure they get it back. I like to pay my debts."

"Sure thing."

Looking down at the dying man beneath them, Malone lifted his eyes and met Damon's gaze. He briefly shook his head, indicating the Texas gunman only had a few, brief moments left to live.

Burns weakly reached his hand forward to touch Malone's arm. "And what might be *your* name, stranger?"

"I'm Kellen Malone."

"Kellen Malone," he said. "I do declare. It's funny the people you meet when you're dead."

Those were the Texan's final words on this earth.

* * * *

"I'm telling you, Walt, I want those nesters gone and off my ranch."

Nothing was said for a moment, as the only sounds in the room were the pops and hisses coming from the blazing wood in the fireplace.

Walt moved the cigar to the edge of his mouth, in order to talk around it. "It's not that simple, Robert. They have women there and there's a kid."

"It'd be pretty simple for me, Pa," Jamie McGregor said. "I'd just burn them out. I told Walt the same thing today."

"And what did Walt say to your idea?"

"He said I was a damned fool, who'd be lucky to see another birthday."

"You said *that*, to *my* son?"

Jamie McGregor smiled to himself, figuring those comments would be the last straw in the career of his father's ranch foreman.

Robert immediately slapped his thigh and threw back his head in a loud and hearty laugh.

"What's so stinking funny about that?" Jamie asked.

"The two of you," McGregor replied. "One of you moves a little too slow for me; the other charges in without even thinking. And both of those ways end up accomplishing nothing." McGregor leaned back in his comfortable desk chair and took another long pull from his cigar. "As bad as I hate to admit it, Walt is absolutely right, Jamie.

"As much as you might want to, you can't just go around killing people to get your way. This country's changing; it's growing up. People won't stand for the old ways so much anymore.

"At the same time, it doesn't mean I'm going to let every wandering sod buster sink his plow into the soil of my ranch, ground that I sweat and bled over to keep."

Walt took a sip of the brandy that was sitting on the edge of the desk in front of him. He savored the taste of the liquor, letting it go down slowly. He followed that up with one more.

"I'll let you handle things your way, Walt, for now. But

make no mistake about it; I want that Coleman family off my ranch before the end of the month.

"Yes, sir."

"You can go now."

Walt picked up the hat from off his lap and headed for the door. "I'll see you in the morning, Robert."

"Thanks, Walt. Have a good evening."

McGregor said nothing more until the door closed behind his ranch foreman.

"And, Jamie, I want you to listen to Walt. He didn't live this long by being stupid."

"Are you calling me stupid?"

"No, I'm not, Jamie. I'm calling you stubborn and ambitious. Those aren't bad qualities for a person to have, but they need to be tempered with patience. Walt has that; you need to learn it.

"I want those nesters gone as much as you do, but we have to go about this thing the right way. Let's give Walt some time and just see how this thing plays out. If he fails to get results, we can always take more drastic measures."

"Okay, Pa. I still don't like it, but I'll try it your way for now."

"Good boy, Jamie. I knew you could see reason. Now that we've got that settled, how about pouring us some more of that fine brandy?"

* * * *

It was long past nightfall before the three outlaws and Burns saw the last shovelfuls of dirt tossed in upon them.

Several hours later, the two strangers were sitting by the fire, sipping coffee and talking, before they turned in for the night.

"It seems to me," Gates said, "that you took great pains *not* to plant Burns' body anywhere near the others."

"I reckon so," Malone replied. "Burns might have been little more than a hired gun. But there at the end, Burns distanced himself from those men. It doesn't seem right that he should be forced to rest beside them in death."

"You're a strange man, Malone."

For the first time, Gates remembered the blood-stained letter he removed from Burns' body. He pulled it from his pocket and opened the letter. The money, $500 in cash, he handed to Malone.

After unfolding the letter Gates stared at the page in silence.

"Go ahead and read it," Malone said.

"I can't."

"Well, then, get over closer to the fire, where you can see it."

"That's not the problem. I can see the words just fine."

Malone was growing impatient. "Then what's the problem?"

"I'm trying to tell you, Mr. Malone. I *can't* read!"

Kell hung his head in shame.

"Growing up on the plantation like I did, nobody was ever allowed to learn us slaves about reading."

"I'm sorry, Damon. I didn't mean anything by it."

"I know you didn't. My Lizzie can read; she's known how for a long time," Gates said, while handing the letter over to

Malone. "Guess I was just too proud to let her learn me, too."

"It's never too late to learn, Damon."

"It is for me."

It only took Malone a few moments to read the contents of the letter. Once finished, Kell refolded the letter, placing it and the money back in the envelope. Then he handed it back to Gates.

"You hang onto this."

The black man stared at the hand writing on the front of the envelope like it was some great treasure, only waiting to be discovered.

"Don't keep me waiting, Mr. Malone. What's it say?"

"The letter came from a rancher named Kane Coleman. The man and his family have a small spread just east of here." Malone took another sip of coffee before he continued. "It seems that their place is smack dab in the middle of another man's claim. That man's name is McGregor."

"Robert McGregor?"

"Yes, that's the name. Do you know him?"

"I know about his son, Jamie McGregor. He threatened to kill a good friend of mine."

"Because he was black?"

"No, it wasn't that. He just wants everybody to know their rightful place. And their rightful place is in the dirt, just under the sole of his boot." Gates stooped beside the fire, rubbing his hands for a little more warmth. "Since his father's the most powerful man in the territory, Jamie figures folks should step aside for him. But what connection do the McGregors have to the man we just buried?"

"As you already know, Burns was a hired gun. And the

$500 dollars was what Coleman paid Burns to keep them living on McGregor's land."

"Are you saying he was going to work for them?"

"No, Damon. He was going to kill for them." Malone reached out and tossed another log in the fire. "It's going to be cold tonight," he added. "The money in that envelope was probably all the savings those people had. But they were willing to pay it, in order to keep McGregor from taking away their land."

"If they're squatting on McGregor's land, Mr. Malone, I can tell you that things will get bad for them. It makes no difference about what Robert McGregor does: Jamie will see to it himself. I wish there was something I could do to help them."

"Returning their money is probably the best thing you could do for them right now. Maybe they can use it to get a start somewhere else."

"You saying they should run?"

"No, Damon. I'm saying they should move."

"What would you do, Mr. Malone, if you was in their place?"

"This isn't about me. It's about them."

"You didn't answer the question, sir. What would *you* do?"

Looking the former slave in the eye, Malone knew the man wasn't going to let the subject drop without a proper answer. "I'd probably stay and fight them for the land. But they're not me."

"So, you're saying that sometimes a piece of land is worth fighting for?"

"Sometimes. I've even done it myself. But you have to remember one thing; this Kane Coleman isn't the only one who'll be fighting for that land. There are still the McGregors."

CHAPTER THREE

AFTER LEAVING HIS FATHER'S OFFICE, JAMIE WENT straight to the bunkhouse.

As he looked around the room, McGregor saw that some of the ranch hands had already turned in for the night. A few of the others were still awake, drinking and playing cards.

Upon seeing it wasn't Walt, a couple of the older men merely sneered at the boss's son and quickly returned to their poker game.

"Scarborough and Yancy!" Jamie shouted. "I need your help."

Yancy grumbled silently, scraped up his meager winnings, and headed for the door. Scarborough never even blinked, instantly laying down his cards since he had no winnings to take with him.

"See you later boys," Alton Davis said. "Make sure you don't forget to give the little one his sugar teat."

All the others, close enough to hear Alton's comment, roared with laughter.

Once the two men were outside, Jamie looked around to

make sure nobody else was around them and close enough to hear.

"I want you two to ride over to the Coleman place tonight."

"What do you want us to do when we get there?" Scarborough asked.

"Oh, I don't know," Jamie replied. "Use your imagination. In any case, I want those squatters out of there.

"Kane Coleman served in a cavalry outfit during the war," Yancy said. "You do know he won't be no pushover, don't you?"

"It really doesn't matter if he's home or not; I want them out. Besides, Walt and I were over there today. There wasn't even any sign of the old man."

Yancy ran his hand through his stubby growth of a beard. The other hand fingered the butt of his Colt. "Come to think of it, I wouldn't mind getting close to the fine looking Coleman woman. I'll bet she can be one spirited filly when she lets her hair down."

"Does Walt know anything about what you have us doing?"

"Listen, Scarborough. You work for me, not Walt!"

'I know that,' Scarborough said. "I wasn't questioning your authority, just trying to read the lay of the land."

"One other thing, there'll be a little something extra in it for the both of you if they're all out of that place by tomorrow."

"Now that kind of talk's more to my liking," Scarborough said. "Why didn't you just say that from the start?"

"And what about the boy?"

"Yancy, don't you worry about the boy," Scarborough replied. "If the money's good, I can handle that end of it."

"I really don't care what you do, but you make good and sure none of it comes back on me. Is that clear?"

"I got you, boss."

"So, then, are you both clear about what I want?"

Both the cowhands nodded.

"By the way, whatever you have to do, I want you back in your bunks when Walt rolls everybody out in the morning."

"Sure enough," Yancy said. "Don't need all night for what I have in mind."

From the moment Jamie first made the offer, Scarborough was still thinking about the promise of something extra. His lips turned up in a smile. "You can count on us, Jamie. We won't disappoint you."

"See that you don't." Jamie removed the watch from his pocket. "You boys better get moving now. Sunrise comes early."

* * * *

BEA COLEMAN HAD LONG SINCE TURNED IN FOR the night when Ann Coleman began preparing for bed. As she finished brushing her hair, Ann was certain she heard the approaching hoof falls of a horse.

Thinking that it must have been Kane, returning from his trip, she rushed to open the door for her sure-to-be weary husband.

Standing outside on the porch, in the glow of the moonlight, were a pair of evil faces, one of them being the McGregor ranch hand who often leered at her in town.

Ann slammed the door, leaning against it with all her strength. However, with Yancy's stronger hand upon it, Ann couldn't manage to get the door fully shut.

She wrestled against the sheer force of the determined outlaw, Ann's back and shoulders an ever-failing barricade against the door. Finally, he reached his arm through the opening, his hand touching her body, moving upward to her face.

Ann bit the man's hand, drawing blood. Yancy screamed out in pain, but the pain and anger only fueled his desire to get inside the house.

With one maddened, evil cry, Yancy lunged forward, throwing open the door and knocking the smaller woman to the floor of the cabin.

He was on top of her in scarcely a moment, groping and tearing at her clothes.

＊＊＊＊

WHILE YANCY MADE HIS FRONTAL ASSAULT ON THE Coleman house, Scarborough rushed around to the side.

Using the butt of his gun for a hammer, he shattered the window pane and tried to climb inside.

As one leg and his head began to enter the window, young Matt had already been awakened by the struggle going on outside his room.

In the darkness of the night, he struck Scarborough in the face with the club he used to hit rocks out back of the ranch house.

The wounded outlaw went sprawling back outside the window.

* * * *

LONG AFTER MALONE WAS ALREADY ASLEEP, DAMON Gates stared at the words on the letter in the flickering glow of the firelight.

Although he couldn't read the words written upon the pages, he thought about the people who wrote them. Gates recognized the need that caused them to write the letter. In addition, the former slave clearly understood the desire to be free from those who were more powerful than himself.

It was the same feeling he'd experienced many a time, while still working in the fields of that Southern plantation.

Most of all, he wanted to do something—anything—to help free them.

After all, Gabriel Burns, the man who'd been hired to help the Coleman family had died while saving *his* life.

Damon felt like he owed that man something as well.

Slowly, a plan began forming in the mind of Damon Gates.

He knew it was crazy, but Gates also knew his mind was made up.

He refolded the letter and returned it to his pocket, as he laid his head down upon the saddle. Gates pulled the blanket up over his shoulders and closed his eyes.

A brief smile came to his lips before he instantly drifted off to sleep.

* * * *

THINKING ONLY OF THE DANGER THAT FACED HER son in the next room, Ann struggled to free herself from the man pulling and tugging at her clothes.

He forced his lips down upon hers in a brutal kiss, the man's foul-smelling breath turning the pits of her stomach.

When Ann bit his lip, Yancy back-handed her across the mouth, the blow nearly knocking the woman into unconsciousness.

Dazed by the blow and knowing exactly what she faced next, Ann feared only what they might do to Matt afterward.

"Now, you and me, we'll have ourselves a little fun," Yancy said. "My boss wants you and your family out of here." His smile was dark and evil, as he once again began clawing at the woman's clothes. "I'm wanting a little of something else."

Inwardly, Ann steeled herself, figuring the only way she could possibly save her son was to somehow endure whatever the man had in mind for her. She saw it as a chance, her only chance.

Just then, the door from Bea's room was thrown open.

Ann's mother-in-law entered the room, her hands holding a shotgun.

Despite her fear and pain, Ann even managed a smile when she saw Matt, safely walking just behind his grandmother.

Upon seeing the woman with the shotgun advancing his way, Yancy climbed off the woman, holding out his hands, and began backing towards the door.

"Now, calm down, ma'am" he said. "It wasn't what it looked like."

Yancy was certain he could talk the old woman into lowering her gun and dropping her guard. Then, after overpowering her and taking the weapon, he and Scarborough would simply finish what they started, leaving no witnesses behind who could tell the story of what happened.

"Mister," Bea replied, "I think it was exactly what it looked like!"

With those words, Bea squeezed both triggers on the double-barrel. The gun roared in her hands, the force bruising her shoulder and blasting Yancy's lifeless body back out through the open door.

Ann quickly scrambled to her feet, softly touching Bea on the shoulder, and hugging her young son.

"Thanks, Bea."

"Glad I could help, Annibel."

As she threw her arms around her son, Ann did her best to hide the fear that she was certain would be showing in her eyes.

"You okay, Ma?"

"I am now, seeing that you're safe."

"Another man tried to come through the window," Matt said. "I hit him."

While Bea fidgeted in her dress pocket to find another couple shotgun shells, Ann raced to the gun rack. She pulled down one of Kane's rifles, levered a shell into the chamber, and rushed into Matt's bedroom.

At the window, she could see a man struggling to mount his horse in the darkness. Ann raised the gun to her shoulder, sighted down the barrel, and fired two quick shots at the man racing away. She had no idea if she hit Scarborough.

When Ann lowered the gun and turned around, a smile greeted her.

In the doorway, Bea stood there, one hand holding a

shotgun, the other around her much-taller grandson.

"I thought you didn't believe in violence, Annibel."

Ann simply smiled. "I don't, but even Quakers love their children."

* * * *

LONG BEFORE THE FIRST RAYS OF SUNLIGHT BEGAN showing over the distant mountains, Walt Jenkins threw open the door to the bunkhouse.

"Come on, boys! It's time to go."

He moved from bunk to bunk, kicking at some, shaking others, all in his attempt to wake the sleeping ranch hands. "Your breakfast is getting cold. Let's go!"

Alton Davis and a couple of the nearly two-dozen hands were already awake. Each of them smiled knowingly, as they watched the ranch foreman go through his daily, morning ritual.

Finally, Walt came to the empty bunks of Yancy and Scarborough.

Walt looked at the sleepy-eyed man in the bunk next to them. "You seen Yancy and Scarborough?"

"Haven't seen them, Walt," the tired cowboy replied, rolling out of bed still fully-clothed, to climb into his boots. "We just got paid yesterday. Maybe they went into town last night to see Maggie."

"They didn't come back last night," Davis added.

"Didn't come back?" Walt asked. "You mean they didn't come back from Maggie's?"

"I don't think they went to spend time with Maggie, Walt."

"So where did they go?"

"Beats me."

"Is that all you've got to say about it?"

"Jamie came and spoke to them last evening."

"Jamie?"

"Yea, Jamie. All I know is they never came back from whatever he sent them out to do. Kind of figured you knew all about it."

"No, I didn't," Walt said. "Don't know about any of it."

"Walt!" a voice yelled out, coming from just outside the bunk house. "You'd better get out here."

When Walt stepped outside, he saw Scarborough's nearly-lifeless body, barely clinging to his horse. Kane Coleman was mounted beside him. A couple of the ranch hands were covering him with their guns.

"Is this one of your men?" Kane asked.

"Well, don't just stand there gawking," Walt replied. "Get him down from that horse and into the bunk house. Cagney, you ride into town for the doc."

"Yes, sir, Boss."

Walt silently watched about four of the men carry the wounded man inside. Then he turned his gaze towards Coleman. "What happened, Kane?"

"I don't know, Walt."

Jenkins looked around at the pair of ranch hands holding guns on Coleman. "You men, put those guns away. Now."

"But this man just rides in here with our friend, shot all to bits," Jake Peters said. "Someone has to pay for that."

"Put the gun away now, Jake! And get on down to breakfast. I can handle things here."

Jake and the other man reluctantly holstered their guns and started walking towards the chuck house. One of the other ranch hands reached out to Kane, returning the man's rifle and pistol.

As Kane returned his guns to their place, the man replied, "They both smell like oil, Walt. Neither of them has been shot for a while."

Walt nodded.

"I've been gone for a few days," Kane said. "Just found him along the trail in the dark. Looks like something bashed in his face and he's got a single bullet hole in his lower back. Your man lost a lot of blood. Be lucky to make through the next hour."

At that moment, the bunk house door opened. "Walt, if Cagney hasn't already left for the doc, don't even bother. Scarborough's dead."

"And you're the one that killed him," a voice among the crowd said.

The voice belonged to Jamie, who was pointing his gun at Coleman. "You knew we wanted you and your family off the ranch, so you just took this chance to kill a couple of our people. I'll see you hang for this."

"What do you mean, a couple of our people? This was the only man I found. What's going on here?"

"I'm wondering about that one, myself," Walt said. "One of my men's dead, Jamie, and you're the last one to see him."

Bitterly, Jamie holstered his gun. "Listen, Coleman, I still want you and your family off our ranch. You understand me?"

With that, he stormed away.

Walt reached up to shake Kane's hand. "Pay no attention to him," he replied. "The boy's stupid. Thanks for bringing our man back here. If you don't mind, I'd like to ride along with you. Maybe you'll take me to the place where you found Scarborough."

Walt looked back towards the ranch hands. "Bring up my horse, will you?" As one of the hands went for his horse, the ranch foreman turned back towards Kane. "It will also give me a chance to talk to you a little."

"Sure thing, Walt, but I doubt you can change my mind."

Walt smiled. "It don't cost nothing to haggle."

* * * *

As Kell was pulling tight the cinch on his saddle, he looked over at the black man, who was just finishing the last of his coffee. "So, Damon, you want me to help you round up those cows before heading home?"

"I'd be much obliged, Mr. Malone." Damon tossed the remainder of his cup on the dwindling coals. "Along the way, I'd like to talk to you about a little something else."

"Be glad to."

"Don't be so quick to speak, Mr. Malone. You might not like my idea after you hears it."

"Fair enough. And like I told you earlier, the name's Kell."

"Yes, sir, Mr. Malone...Kell, I mean."

"Now that's more like it. By the way," Kell said, "if you don't mind me asking, where is home for you?"

"It's just outside of a town called Nicodemus."

Chapter Four

As the two men rode along, Kane pointed to the place where he'd earlier found Scarborough's body. "It's right over there."

Walt and Kane drew rein at the spot.

"Pretty good blood trail he left," Walt said. "Shouldn't be too hard to follow it."

"What's that you said about another one of your men missing?"

"Darrell Yancy. He partners with Scarborough, or he did."

The pair of riders followed the trail on horseback, only occasionally leaving their mounts to pick up some additional sign.

"This doesn't look good."

"What do you mean?"

"I think you know darn well what I'm talking about, Walt. This trail looks like it's headed for my place. What did your men come out here for?"

"I don't know."

"You sure about that?"

"Of course I'm sure. I said so, didn't I?"

Realizing that the wounded man's blood trail could lead only to his place, Kane spurred his horse into a gallop for home. Quickly catching up to the other horse, Walt's mount matched him stride-for-stride.

Just outside his house, Kane jumped from the saddle, scarcely allowing the horse to come to a stop. There, he saw his mother washing blood from the porch with soap and a bucket of fresh water.

"Are you okay, Ma?"

"Yes, I'm fine, son. We had ourselves a little trouble last night."

Saying nothing further, Kane embraced the dear woman who gave him life. "What about Ann? And Matt?"

"None the worse for wear," she said. Satisfied his mother was okay, Kane raced into the house.

Just then, the door opened, bringing him face-to-face with the still-frightened eyes of his wife. The woman rushed forward to meet Kane, throwing her arms around her husband. Ann's lips rose to meet his.

"You're okay now," Kane said. "I'm here."

Upon seeing Matt, Kane pulled away from Ann and went to hug his son. "Matt. Are you okay, son?"

"Sure, Pa. I'm fine."

"What happened here?" Kane asked.

* * * *

OUTSIDE THE HOUSE, WALT PAUSED TO LOOK AT the woman who was finishing her chore of cleaning the last of Yancy's blood from the porch.

The ranch foreman saw Beatrice to be an attractive woman and figured them to be about the same age. But then, he immediately questioned his first evaluation, always doubting himself in all things regarding the fairer sex.

When their eyes met, Walt fumbled to remove his hat. "Were you the one at the window yesterday, pointing the gun at me?"

Bea smiled. "Wasn't sure you saw me."

"Yea, I saw you, ma'am."

"Bet you can't say the same for the kid who rode with you."

Walt threw back his head with laughter. "No, I guess I can't. It's not likely Jamie McGregor will ever have the smarts to live as long as the two of us."

"Not to say you're old, ma'am. I just meant. You see, I was just trying to say. Well, no offense meant to you."

Bea simply smiled. "None taken."

"May I ask what happened here?"

"A pair of men came here late last night. Better still, make that early this morning. Come with me," Beatrice said, making her way towards the barn. "Figured they must have been a couple of your ranch hands."

"Yes, they were, ma'am, sorry to say."

"Is that your man over there, underneath the blanket?"

Walt sauntered over to the body, knelt beside him, and lifted the cover from the man's face. "Yep, that's Yancy."

"Real bad man, that one," she said. "Tried to molest Annibel. The other one, he tried to come through my grandson's room. He got away."

"Begging your pardon, ma'am, but no, he didn't. We found him, or your son in there did. He died this morning. Lost too much blood, I think."

"Can't say I'm sorry to hear that."

"Can't say I blame you much, ma'am. Man caught harming a woman or a child, I'd probably kill him myself." Walt looked the woman in the eyes. "I trust you'll believe me on this; I'd never knowingly have a man like that working for me."

"I believe you."

Just about that time, Kane threw open the barn door. Walking towards the ranch foreman with an ever-quickening pace, Kane threw a roundhouse right hand at Walt's left jaw.

The ranch foreman went to the floor like he'd been kicked by a mule.

"What are you doing, Kane?" Beatrice said.

"Stop it, Kane! Stop it now!" Ann said, rushing behind her husband into the barn.

Kane pointed his finger at the man in the straw beneath them. "So your boss couldn't get us to leave and you let a couple of your outlaws come out here to harm my wife and family." Kane drew his gun, pointing it at the man he'd just struck. "I ought to kill you, Walt. I ought to kill you, right here and now. Then I ought to kill your boss."

"Stop it, Kane!" Ann said. Her eyes blazed at him beneath the bonnet she wore on her head. "And put that gun away! My gracious! Don't you think there's been enough killing here already?"

Grudgingly, Kane holstered his gun.

"I didn't have anything to do with this," Walt said, coming to his feet as he dusted himself off. "Nothing at all."

"Coming home, finding this here, thinking about what happened—guess I just lost my head." Kane stuck out his hand to the ranch foreman. "No hard feelings?"

Walt paused to rub his jaw before taking the man's hand. "No hard feelings, just sore ones."

Kane put his arm around Matt, as the two of them made their way outside.

Annibel picked up the fallen man's hat and handed it to Walt.

"Thanks."

"You'll have to forgive my son. He can be a little head-strong at times. Must have gotten that from his father."

"That's okay, ma'am. If harm came to my family's door like this, it might make me a little crazy, too."

"So," Bea asked, "do you have a family?"

"No, I don't. Guess I never met the right woman."

"That surprises me."

"Really? How so, ma'am?"

"I would think there'd be no shortage of ladies interested in a tall, handsome fellow like you."

Walt's face turned at least a half-dozen shades of red. "That's kind of you to say, ma'am."

Listening to their conversation, Ann suddenly felt out of place, like she'd ventured into the middle of something private. She stared at Beatrice in disbelief.

Ann had never seen Bea appear to be so forward with a man; it was a side of her mother-in-law she'd never seen before. Ann fussed with her dress, fiddled with the strings to her bonnet, and finally scurried towards the door.

"Please forgive my lack of good manners, ma'am," he said, with a slight tip of the hat. "My name's Walt Jenkins."

"Why, it's certainly a pleasure, sir. My name is Beatrice Coleman, but most people call me Bea."

"Beatrice, that's a lovely name."

"Well, I'm glad you like it, Walt. Then you'll feel free to use it when you take me to the town dance, come next Saturday night."

Walt was shocked at the woman's direct nature. On second thought, though, he found it kind of refreshing. In addition, he also found Beatrice to be an attractive and unusual woman.

"You said it yourself, Walt; we're about the same age. People of *our* age don't have time for well-meaning acts of formal tradition. I like to dance and I've just found out it's a whole lot easier with two."

Walt smiled. "I'd be honored to escort you to the dance, Beatrice. See you about four o'clock then?"

"Sounds lovely."

As the two of them started outside the barn, Walt blushed as Beatrice placed her arm inside his. The veteran cowhand quickly warmed to the idea of her arm on his. Walt briefly caught the scent of her, a smell much more pleasant than those to which he was normally accustomed.

When the two of them exited the barn, Ann scowled at the sight of them arm-in-arm. Kane saw it too, leaving him only bewildered.

Reluctantly, Walt removed his arm from the woman's grasp to climb atop his horse. "Listen, Kane. You can be sure that I'll get to the bottom of what happened here."

"I know you probably don't have any reason to trust me right now, but I'm certain Robert McGregor had nothing to do with this."

"What about Jamie?"

"That there's a good question, Kane. And I aim to find out. One thing you can count on, you'll hear from me soon. And, if you'll allow it, I'll send a couple of the boys over later today, to pick up Yancy's body."

Kane nodded.

With a glance down at Beatrice Coleman, Walt said, "Mrs. Coleman, sorry about the circumstances, but it's been a real pleasure. Reckon I'll see you next Saturday."

At those words, the others turned and went back into the house.

"Before riding off, I have to know one thing."

"What's that, Mr. Jenkins?"

"At the window yesterday, would you really have shot me?"

"I shot Yates."

"Guess I'd better treat you right then. Wouldn't be healthy to trifle with a woman who just killed two men."

"I didn't kill two men, Mr. Jenkins. Annibel, the angry, Quaker woman shot the other one. And your people need to know one other thing, Mr. Jenkins."

"What's that?"

"It isn't healthy to harm the child of an armed woman who's prone to non-violence."

Walt just laughed. "I'll be sure to pass that one along. Good day, Mrs. Coleman."

As Jenkins started down the trail for home, the woman

was certain she heard the foreman softly whistling a tune.

* * * *

As Malone checked the cinch on his horse's saddle, he threw a quick glance toward Gates. "Since I'm already here, you want me to help you round up those cows and push them back towards your place?"

Gates nodded, while he kicked dirt over the last of the fire. "Be much obliged if you would."

"I'll be glad to do it then," Kell said with a smile. "Seeing as how you almost paid for them with your life, I don't see any reason why you shouldn't keep their horses. I'll write you up a paper, telling how you came to have them. We'll get it witnessed by the marshal in the next town."

Still sipping the last of his coffee from the cup, Damon Gates walked over to where Malone was saddling his horse. "I don't mean to pry, Mr. Malone, but I've heard of you before. Folks say you're mighty good with a gun."

"Lots of men are good with a gun, Damon. And I thought I told you to call me Kell."

"Sorry, Kell. Still ain't used to calling a man by his first name. Hard to break old habits I learned back on the plantation." Damon drained the last of his coffee, shook out the cup, and stuck it back into his saddlebag. "Guess I can't argue with what you're saying, but there's still a difference. Lots of men may be good with a gun, but not too many of them walked away from the gunfights you've had."

Kell suddenly stopped what he was doing and stared across the saddle at the former slave. "Sometimes, when a man has something big on his mind, it's best to just come out with it."

"I know it's none of my concern, but how does a man get to be real good with a gun, like you and Gabriel Burns?"

"I can't speak for Burns, but in my case, I had no choice." Silently, Malone leaned on his horse for a brief moment, his mind recalling an ancient memory. "Many years ago, a man outside our house pulled iron on my pa. I think I was only about twelve at the time. Don't even remember why I was wearing a holster gun at the time; probably young and stupid. Might have been out hunting.

"All I really remember is what happened next. Pa wasn't armed. The man figured to shoot him down in cold blood. My only shot knocked him clean out of the saddle and he hit the ground dead.

"Hoping to protect me, Pa tried to claim he was the one who did the shooting. Only trouble with that was, a neighbor saw the whole thing from the hill above us. Then, after he had a couple of drinks in the saloon, everybody in town knew about it.

"The man I killed was considered to be pretty handy with a gun. To make matters worse, he had two older brothers who were better. Pa packed up some things for me, saddled up his best horse, and told me to ride for the hills. Little more than a few months later, I was wearing the Union blue."

"Can a person practice enough to get good with a gun, like you, I mean?"

"I suppose you could," Malone said, pushing back his hat and scratching his forehead. "Why do you want to know?"

Damon shrugged. "I'm still thinking about the letter that Burns had. It kept me awake most of the night. I don't really care about the money much, but the person who wrote that letter needed help. Burns was headed that way when he stopped to help me."

"It's too bad about Burns. But you're not to blame for his death, Damon."

"No, I'm not. That was his own decision to help; I know that. But I *am* to blame for the fact those people won't have a gunman riding to their aid. I can't get them out of my mind. What will become of *them*? What if Burns was the only hope they had?"

"I understand that," Malone said. "But what does any of this have to do with you?"

Damon caught the saddle horn with his left hand and swung himself up into the saddle. He cast a quick glance over at Malone. "They need help, Kell, and I want to go in Gabriel's place. And I'd like you to teach me how to shoot."

Malone shook his head in bewilderment. "I'm not sure if you're noble or just stupid. Don't you realize that you almost lost your life yesterday? A man lucky enough to have his life spared shouldn't go around trying to throw it away."

"Maybe my life was spared for a reason."

"You mean like going home to your wife and family?" Kell asked.

"No, I mean like trying to help someone else get a second chance at life."

Malone shook out the reins, spurred his horse, and started down the trail. Damon Gates quickly eased his horse alongside him.

"Will you help me, Kell?"

"You sure there's no way I can talk you out of this?"

"No, there isn't. I'm going to do it anyway, with or without your help."

"I have to tell you, Damon, this all goes against my better judgment. I'll probably be responsible for getting you killed."

"Well, look at it this way, Kell. If you don't help me, I'm almost certain to get killed. And since I already asked you for your help, it *is* certain you'll be responsible for that one."

Upon hearing his statement, Kell quickly drew rein. He looked over at the black man who was riding beside him.

"You did tell me that you were a slave back there in the South, didn't you?"

"Sure, I did. Why'd you ask?"

Kell removed his canteen, taking a long pull of water before speaking.

"After seeing the game you just run on me, I figured anybody as crafty as you had to end up running the place."

Chapter Five

Robert McGregor gave Jamie a slap that rattled his skull.

"What was that for, Pa? I thought you said you wanted them out of there."

"I do."

"So, what's your problem with what I did?"

"Sure, I wanted Coleman and his wife off my land, but I also told you to be smart about it. Not only did you get two of our best men killed, you've made it even harder for us to do anything more about Coleman and his family. Now, if we have to kill them, it will look like we picked the fight. We'll be mighty lucky if we can keep the law out of this mess."

Jamie rubbed the red mark on his jaw. "But there's something else, Pa. I'm hearing rumors that Coleman has been out there trying to find a hired gun."

"A hired gun, huh?"

"Yes, a hired gun."

"Mmm, now that's the sort of information that just might have worked to our advantage." He paused long enough to glare at his son. "In fact, that's the sort of information you should have shared with me from the start, Jamie. Now, it looks like the only option left for me is to leave them there."

"Leave them there!"

"Yes, leave them. That's the price we pay for you being stupid."

"You mean there's nothing else we can do?"

"Not without someone bringing in the law."

"But you own the sheriff."

"I'm not talking about him. Something like this could cause the governor to get involved, maybe causing him to send in a U.S. Marshal. We don't need that.

"Look, Jamie, we've got more than enough hands on this ranch to kill Kane Coleman or to run them off. But we have to be able to live around here after they're gone. People hear things; people talk. And there's a couple of women and a child involved. That makes it lot harder to run roughshod over them.

"There's plenty of good reasons why a law-abiding rancher might have to kill a man. It gets tougher when women and children figure into the mix. Yep, the more I think about it, the more it becomes clear to me. We have to let those squatters stay."

"But what about the gunman they're trying to hire?"

"Looks to me like they've gone and wasted their money for nothing." The wealthy rancher managed a hearty laugh. "If we're lucky, maybe it was the money Coleman needed to plant next year's crops.

"After they've had a few days to settle down from this latest incident, Walt and I will ride over there and clean up the damage. Between now and then, just don't do anything to make the situation worse than it already is. Can I get your word on that?"

"Sure, Pa. I swear I won't do anything at all until you've talked to them, not since it sounds like your mind is made up."

"It is, son. There's a couple of ways you can handle this, Jamie. You can let this whole thing get your back up or you can look at it as a learning experience."

"I'll definitely look at it as a learning experience, Pa."

"That's good, Jamie. I'm sure you already know that, one of these days, this whole place will be yours. You need to learn how to deal with these things. Sometimes circumstances cause you to adjust your methods."

* * * *

"Lizzie, I want you to meet my friend, Kellen Malone."

"I am honored, Mr. Malone."

"Please call me Kell." Malone gently tipped his hat and shook the woman's outstretched hand. "It's nice to know you, ma'am."

"Okay, sir, I will call you Kell, but only if you'll call me Lizzie."

"It's a deal, Lizzie."

"Please, Kell, sit down here at the table next to Damon. May I get you a cup of coffee?" She said, pouring from the pot before even receiving his response.

"I'd be very grateful," Kell said, removing his hat and placing it on a chair beside him.

48

"I'll take that for you," said the voice of an aged black woman, who just entered from another room of the cabin.

Kell immediately rose to his feet.

"Kell, this is my mother, Tess. Ma, this is Kellen Malone."

"Pleased to meet you, Tess."

"Same here, Mr. Malone. Go ahead and sit back down," Tess said. She hung his hat from a peg on the wall and then chose a seat directly across from him.

As Malone sipped his coffee, the old woman's piercing eyes studied the tall stranger for a time. "You sure don't look like the vicious killer that I heard tell of."

Damon and Lizzie were shocked by the woman's statement.

"What kind of thing is that for you to say, Ma? This man is a guest in our home."

"No offense taken," Kell said. "It's one of the things I've always admired about older folks; they tend to say whatever's on their minds."

"Thank you, Mr. Malone," Tess said. "But before I was cut off, I also wanted to say that, despite that pair of matched guns you're wearing, you have the look of a man who can be trusted. I'm proud my son made your acquaintance."

"Why thank you very much, ma'am."

"And very well-mannered, too. I like that."

Kell just smiled.

"From what I hear from Damon," Lizzie said, "we are all greatly in your debt for saving my husband's life."

"I didn't do much. The man who really saved Damon's life, Gabriel Burns, we buried him back on the trail."

"He's being way too modest. That noose was choking the

last bit of life out of me," Damon said. "There's probably not a dozen men in the West who could have made that shot. Lucky for me, Kell's one of them."

Tess smiled and looked at Malone. "Sounds like my read on you is right after all."

"And," Damon added, "Kell helped me to gather up the cows I bought and herd them back here. After those men tried to hang me, those cows were scattered to here and gone. All by myself, might have been a week getting them all together."

Malone took another sip of his coffee. "Just glad I could help."

"Well, it's getting late and you and the mister have an early day ahead of yourselves tomorrow. Kell, you're welcomed to toss your bedroll right here in front of the fire," Lizzie said.

"I'd be much obliged."

"You need anything?"

"No, thanks, Lizzie. I'm good here."

"Okay, then. We'll all be turning in for the night. See you in the morning."

"Good night, folks," he said.

Malone started to make his bed there on the floor. Once satisfied, he blew out the lamp and climbed underneath his blanket. His head scarcely hit his saddlebags before he drifted off to sleep.

* * * *

"Damon," she said, "are you sure you want to do this?"

"I have to, Lizzie. Burns saved my life when he was on his

way to help others." Damon tried to move quickly, pulling on his clothes and shoving some things in a bag. "You saw the letter. What if those people have nobody else to help them?"

"What if we have nobody else, because you go and get yourself killed?"

The two of them tried to keep their voices down, so as not to be overheard by the man who was starting to rustle around in the next room.

"Is Malone going with you?"

"For a little while, anyways. Kell promised to teach me how to use a gun. Don't know what he'll do after that."

"Then, why doesn't he just do it himself?"

"It's not his fight."

"It's not yours either."

"It wasn't his life that was saved by Gabriel Burns, a man who could've just let me swing." Damon softly took his wife in his arms and pulled her closer to him. "Then I'd be dead and those people in the letter wouldn't be all alone, just like you'd have been, if I was still swinging on that tree."

He pulled the woman closer to him and softly kissed her on the lips. "I know you, Lizzie. That isn't something you'd want for yourself and it isn't something you'd want for anybody else."

The woman playfully slapped him on the shoulder. "Damon Gates, I hate it when you do that to me."

"What do you mean?"

"I hate it when you're right." Lizzie reached up to kiss the man she loved. "Your mother and I will be all right here. You go and try to help those people and then you hurry home to us. Do you hear me? You hurry back to us."

"Yes, ma'am."

When the two of them left their bedroom, they saw that Malone and Tess were already awake. Malone had both of their horses saddled and Tess had prepared breakfast for them all.

For the first time, Malone noticed the young boy sitting at the table. "You must have been sleeping when I got here last night. And what is your name, son?" Malone said, sticking out his hand.

The boy returned his handshake. "I am Jacob."

"Pleased to meet you, Jacob. You can call me Kell."

Lizzie interrupted them. "Jacob, you can call him *Mr. Kell!*"

Malone smiled sheepishly. "Sorry, ma'am. Maybe you better call me mister, son."

"Are you the man that helped save my daddy?"

"I didn't do all that much. Most everything was over when I got there."

The boy smiled. "Thanks for bringing him home, Mister Kell."

"It was my pleasure, son."

Not much was said around the table as Damon ate what his family thought might be his last meal in their meager home. Sensing their mood, Malone said very little, only politely commenting on the food or responding to the statements of others. Lizzie was the first one to rise from the table, quickly preparing some food and biscuits for the two men to take on their journey.

"Thank you very much for your kindness," Malone said, tipping his hat to the two women. He quickly stepped outside, giving Damon some last moments of privacy with his loved ones.

Tess followed Malone outside the small, but comfortable, sod house.

"Mr. Malone," she said, "I don't know what twist of fate brought you into our lives, but you're here now. I guess I have to ask. Why are you doing this, helping my son, I mean?"

"He asked me to."

"Is that all it takes?"

"It was with him." Kell said, swinging himself up into the saddle. Then he leaned forward on the saddle horn, speaking to the woman below. "You have to understand that men like your son are rare in this world, Mrs. Gates. I've not met many like him. Saw a number of them cut down in the war. It'd be a shame to see the world lose any more."

"You are truly a strange man, Mr. Malone."

Kell merely laughed. "Sounds like you and my wife have been talking."

"No, I mean it. I've never known too many men who would risk their life for a total stranger. It's something truly special, or rare, as you call it. My precious Ben was that way before he died. So is Damon. And so are you, Mr. Malone."

"That's kind of you to say."

"You take good care of my son."

"I'll do my best."

"I'm sure you will." Tess Gates walked over towards Malone's horse, handing him up the small bag of provisions. "These might come in handy on the trail."

"Thank you, Mrs. Gates."

"I will pray for Damon. And for you."

About that time, Damon, Lizzie, and Jacob came out of the house. Damon briefly kissed his wife one more time and took a moment to hug his mother and son.

"You ready to ride, Kell?"

"Sure, I am. I was hoping you'd change your mind."

"No chance."

"Mister Kell," Jacob said, "please bring my daddy home safe."

Malone smiled and nodded. "I'll do my best." Then he tipped his hat and reined his horse around.

Damon lingered for only a moment, taking one final look at his beloved family, before he spurred his horse to catch up with Malone.

During those times when warriors are confronted with the greatest dangers, they often put on their bravest faces for the ones they love. And during those times, the ones they love often do the same.

Tess moved over to place her arm around her daughter-in-law's shoulder.

"Go with God," Lizzie said. "Go with God."

* * * *

FROM THE HILLSIDE, THE MAN LOOKED DOWN AT the road, cursed softly, and ground his fifth cigarette under the heel of his boot. He'd been waiting several hours; he would be willing to wait several more.

The man removed his hat, wiping the sweat from his forehead with his shirt sleeve. He brushed the dust from his clothes. He tried to find a better position in which to hunker down. He took another gulp of water from his canteen.

None of it made him more comfortable or made the time pass more quickly.

Since this was their only route home, he knew the riders would eventually come this way. Despite the fact that patience had never been one of his few virtues, he determined to be here when they did.

For nearly the hundredth time, the man checked his rifle. Then he built another cigarette and realized it would be the last of his makings.

* * * *

"THAT WAS A REAL GOOD THING YOU DID BACK there, boss, agreeing to let Coleman and his family stay on your ranch. You said some nice things to them, too." Walt Jenkins cast a knowing and doubtful eye at Robert McGregor. "How many of those things did you really mean?"

The pair of riders had ridden only about fifteen minutes down the trail from the Coleman place. A hot meal would be waiting for them back at McGregor's ranch house.

McGregor just laughed. "Anybody else asked me that question, I'd probably pull a gun and shoot them. You're the only man I know who could get away with it."

"You and me riding together again, boss. It seems like old times."

"Yes, it does. I don't do this enough. We crossed a lot of rivers back then, fought a lot of battles, and shed a little blood together. I don't think I could have built this great ranching empire without you, Walt."

"Then I'm glad you didn't listen to Jamie and put the whole thing at risk for a few squatters. You *do* know it had to be him who sent Yates and Scarborough over to the Coleman place, don't you?"

"Of course I know. Who else could it have been?"

"What do you plan to do about it?"

"What I just did, or what we just did."

"Is that all?"

"What more can I do, Walt? It won't bring those men back. The Coleman women were scared and threatened, but didn't suffer any lasting harm. And I don't want to see my boy punished for one stupid and thoughtless act.

"Since you don't have any children of your own, Walt, you probably can't fully understand what I'm saying. A man will often protect his child from the consequences of his actions, even when it isn't in the child's best interest to do so."

"Guess I'll have to take your word on that one, boss."

"Yes, you will. Come on, Walt. Let's pick up the pace. Don't know about you, but I'm getting a little hungry."

Chapter Six

After the two men had ridden for awhile, Damon noticed they weren't headed towards Colorado. Although he'd made note of their direction several times, he'd chosen to remain silent.

But upon seeing the town of Paradise Flats just ahead of them, Gates could no longer hold his peace.

"I hate to second-guess you, Kell, but I'm pretty certain we're not headed in the direction of Colorado. You mind telling me where we're going?"

"Not at all. I've watched you checking our direction for the last twenty miles, Damon. Guess I was just curious when you'd get around to asking the question I knew was on your mind."

"Well, why didn't you say something?"

Malone simply smiled. "I figured that was up to you."

"My ma taught me to never grumble at a man who was doing me a favor."

Upon entering the town, Malone tipped his hat to a pair of men sitting outside a building on the north end of town.

They nodded back towards the stranger and quickly returned to their conversation.

"Real good woman, your ma. And generally I'd agree with her, but not this time. When a man is willing to risk his life for people that he's never met," Kell said, speaking in low tones so as not to be heard by the townspeople, "that quality alone buys you the right to ask me just about anything at any time."

"Okay, Kell. I'm asking. What are we doing in Paradise Flats?"

"I have to see a man about a gun."

"Lots of places west of here sell guns."

"But not too many of their owners won't ask a lot of questions about why I'm buying a gun for a black man." Malone suddenly drew rein in front of a store. "This one won't."

"What makes you think I can't pay for it by myself?"

"Cause you spent about all the extra money you had on buying those cows."

"Who in the world told you that?"

"You just did."

"You think you're pretty smart, don't you, Kellen Malone? You can be certain I'll pay you back."

"Not if they kill you first."

"Then you'd better do a good job of teaching me."

"It's an easy thing to teach a man to kill, Damon. But no amount of teaching will guarantee a man won't die once he enters into a war."

Malone threw a couple of turns of the reins around the hitch rail as Damon followed his lead. The two men ducked under the rail and went inside the store.

The storekeeper had installed a tiny bell, which rang whenever customers entered the place. Upon hearing the sound, the elderly storekeeper made his way to the front of the store.

"Why, Kellen Malone!" he said, throwing his arms around the much-taller man. "And just how in the world are you doing, boy?"

"Just fine!" he said, "Denny Abrams, this here is my friend, Damon Gates, from up around Nicodemus."

"Yea, I know the place. That's a Colored town, isn't it?"

Gates nodded.

"I met some nice people on my only visit through there, when my horse came up lame," he replied, offering his hand to Damon. "And any friend of Kell's is certainly welcomed in my place."

Upon hearing the word "friend," Damon threw a curious glance at Malone. It was the first time he recalled any white man ever using that word in reference to him.

"What can I do you for?"

"Mr. Gates here is needing a gun."

"I think we can fix him up right up, Kell." He started walking towards the back of the store. "Please follow me, gentlemen. Long gun or a Colt?"

Denny walked around behind the counter to where all the guns were displayed. Then he pointed toward all the choices available to them.

"Short gun," Kell replied. "And a holster."

"You want a new one, Kell, or are you looking for something second-hand?"

"If a man's life depends on his gun, then it doesn't make

any sense for him to go second-rate. Make it a new shooter. But not the holster, Denny. I want that to have a little wear to it."

"Wise choice, Kell."

Gates said nothing as he simply stared at all the bright, new, and shiny hardware right there before him. Damon never owned a new gun; he'd never owned anything new. The closest he came were the new items of clothing made for him from second-hand scraps of fabric.

"Go ahead, Damon. Pick one out."

Unaware that anyone had spoken to him, the black man continued to stare at the dozens of shiny guns.

"Mr. Gates," Denny said, "which one do you want?"

Finally realizing what the shopkeeper had said, Damon's eyes danced from one gun to the other. Unsure of which one to pick, Damon looked over toward Malone for some guidance.

"Nobody knows more about guns than you do, Kell. Which one would you pick?"

Kell quickly looked over the guns in the case and pointed to the one in the corner. "How about that one?"

"Good choice," Denny said, removing the gun from the case. "Try it out, Damon. See how it feels in your hand."

Damon reached out for the gun like it was a rattle snake.

"Go ahead, Damon," Kell said. "Get the heft of it."

Gates finally took the gun from the storekeeper's hand. But once he laid hold upon it, Damon believed it was just about the most beautiful thing he'd ever seen.

He turned it over in his hand, watching the light reflect off the new steel barrel. Damon opened the cylinder and listened to each of the six metallic clicks.

"How does it fit your hand?"

Gates smiled. "It feels like it was made for it."

Denny handed the black man a second-hand holster, which, this time, Damon didn't hesitate to accept.

He quickly strapped on the belt and holstered the gun. The new gun felt sort of heavy on his right hip.

"Is that the one you want?"

"Yea, Kell. Thank you. This one will be just fine."

"You heard the man, Denny. Figure out what I owe you."

"Give the gun and holster back to Denny and let him wrap it up."

"Give it back?" Damon asked, reluctantly handing the gun to the storekeeper.

"Just for a minute, Mr. Gates. I'll wrap up the gun and the holster and hand them right back to you."

"Oh, okay."

Once the man wrapped up the gun and holster, into a neat, brown paper package, he handed the gun to Gates, who clutched it to him like a child with a new puppy.

"Thank you, sir," Gates said. "It's a pleasure to meet you."

"Same here, Mr. Gates."

As Damon left the place, Malone counted out the money for the gun, and handed it over to storekeeper. Denny reached down and took four boxes of cartridges from the counter and handed them to Malone.

"You'll probably need this ammo, Kell. I'm throwing them in the deal."

Kell smiled and nodded as he took them. "Thanks, Denny. It's been good to see you again."

"Same here, Kell. Ride careful."

The two of them shook hands.

"The next time you show up here, you make sure you bring that pretty little wife, Rachel, with you. She's a whole lot easier on the eyes than your old horse face."

"Can't argue with you there. See you, Denny."

Gates was waiting in front of the store when Malone came out the door. The former slave was still firmly clutching the brand new gun as he waited next to his horse.

"You ready to ride, Damon?"

"Sure I am, Kell. But about the gun, why did we have to wrap it up? I could have just left it on, like you're wearing yours."

"I reckon you can consider this our first lesson. "

"Our first lesson?"

"Yes, Damon. The minute you strap that gun around your hip, at that very moment, you become an armed man. Anybody could push you into a fight, for any reason. And since you were already armed, they can draw iron on you." Kell loosed his reins and swung himself up into the saddle. "And right now, with no more ability than you'd have with that gun, Lizzie would be a widow."

Malone spurred his horse out of town.

Damon smiled while looking at the package one more time. Then he shoved it in his saddlebags and followed Malone out of town.

* * * *

ON THE HILLTOP ABOVE THE ROAD, THE MAN WAS still waiting. His final cigarette was long-since gone; his patience was exhausted long before he ran out of smokes.

Then, he saw the riders coming.

Finally!

The man lifted the rifle to his shoulder, sighted down the barrel to a spot on the man's back, and coolly squeezed the trigger. The gun leaped in his hands as the rider was loosed from his saddle.

He levered another shell into the chamber, took careful aim, and blasted the second man from his now-running horse.

Once more, the man removed his hat and wiped his brow, staring down at the scene stretched out before him. He holstered his rifle and took another long pull from his canteen. The frown on his face soon became a smile.

Two shots fired, two men down. Even pa would have been proud. Maybe it was worth the long wait, after all.

* * * *

"Isn't that good news, Kane? Now there won't have to be any more bloodshed for us to stay on this land," Ann said.

"It's good news if he means it."

"What makes you think he wouldn't?"

"Experience."

"But, Kane, how can you be that skeptical of the generous promise the man made to us. Perhaps God has answered my prayers."

"Perhaps God had nothing to do with it! I think it's much more likely that McGregor's trying to get us to let our guard down, or to send Burns away when he arrives," Kane said. "One thing's for certain, whatever his plans might be, you can bet they have nothing to do with *our* best interests."

"Well, I think the man was sincere."

"You're a Quaker, Ann. You think everybody's sincere. Have you forgotten that McGregor sent two men over to this house to kill you? And maybe worse!"

"But we don't know that was Robert McGregor. It could have been his son."

"Not much difference in the two of them, if you ask me."

While listening to their conversation, Beatrice had said nothing as she sipped her coffee. Finally, it became too much for her to remain a silent party. "I don't trust Robert or Jamie McGregor any farther than I can throw them, but I don't believe Walt Jenkins would be a party to a scheme designed to harm us."

Kane simply scowled at the woman who gave him birth. "I'm sorry, Ma, but going to one town dance together doesn't mean you really know the man."

Ann laughed. "Oh, really, Kane? One town dance was all it took for me to know you."

"Okay! Okay, already! I give up. Ain't no one man going to win a conversation with two women. But I'll tell you this. Only a fool lays down his guns just because the wealthy and powerful say they mean you no harm. And Gabriel should be here any day now."

"Gabriel?"

"Yes, Gabriel Burns."

"Gabriel, one of the Lord's highest angels, it's a strange name for a killer."

"Sounds like a good name to me," Kane said. "Maybe

64

Gabriel Burns will put the fear of God into the McGregors."

"That's blasphemous talk, Kane. I will hear no more of it from you."

"Listen, Ann, we'll see what happens in the next few days. If things stay quiet until Burns arrives, we can make a decision then. Until then, you can trust the Lord; I will put my trust in Samuel Colt."

"Must there always be a world with so many guns?"

"Yes, Annibel," Beatrice said. "There must always be guns as long as there's a world that knows so much evil."

Kane grabbed his hat and his rifle and started for the front door. "Amen to that."

* * * *

THE MAN DISMOUNTED HIS HORSE AND PALMED HIS gun, before checking on the two men he'd just shot from the hilltop.

Carefully and slowly, he walked over to the first man. He could see the bullet hole in the back of the man's vest. Blood was pooling all around the body. He kicked the man in the ribs and then raked him with the rowel of his spur. He didn't even get a grunt of pain.

The man had to be dead already.

Then he walked over to the other man, stooping down to roll over the body. The wounded man's eyes opened. Upon seeing the one kneeling over him, he was suddenly hopeful of being rescued.

"Jamie, I'm so glad to see you, boy. Somebody ambushed us from the hill."

Jamie smiled. "Yea, it was me, Pa. Remember our chat

from the other day? I told you I wouldn't do a thing until you talked to them. Well, you've talked now."

Robert McGregor was bewildered.

"Why would you shoot us, son? Why would you shoot me?"

"To tell you the truth, I never liked Walt Jenkins, anyway. That one I'd have simply taken on for fun. But you, Pa, you were simply business. Nothing personal. You're probably thirsty. Let me get you a drink."

Jamie walked over to his horse, removing the canteen from his saddle. As he walked back towards his father, he took one more look at Walt Jenkins' body, looking for any sign of life. He smiled once again as he saw none.

Kneeling beside his father's body, he lifted Robert's head, putting the canteen to his lips. After a couple of swallows of the cool, clear water, Jamie eased his father's head to the ground once more. Then he continued his story.

"The great and mighty Robert McGregor and his ranch foreman ride out to talk peace with Kane Coleman. The two of them seem to reach to an agreement. That's why it made no sense for Coleman to shoot down the two of them like dogs.

"Terrible thing, really. Shocking to all the townspeople. Who would have ever expected such a thing from those God-fearing Coleman folks? It's the kind of crime that just screams out for some kind of justice."

McGregor couldn't believe the words he was hearing. "But, Jamie, why would you do this?"

"It's like you told me, Pa. Sometimes circumstances cause you to adjust your methods. You remember saying that to me? Pretty sound thinking it was; I've got to give you that."

Despite his shock, Robert was beginning to accept the gravity of his situation and to fear what else might be in store for him.

"What happens now, son?"

"You know I can't just leave you here, Pa. You might live; you might talk. Of course that would spoil all my plans."

"So you just plan to shoot me, in cold blood?"

"I guess I'm a little hurt that you think it might be that easy for me. This wasn't an easy decision to come to, Pa. I hope you appreciate that fact."

"My god, boy. What happened to you?"

"Like I said, Pa, don't take it so hard. Remember what else you taught me? There's a couple of ways you can handle this, Pa. You can let this whole thing get your back up or you can look at it as a learning experience."

The words had scarcely left his lips before Jamie McGregor palmed his gun and placed two shots in the body of his father.

"A learning experience," he said. "I kind of like that."

Jamie threw his canteen over his shoulder and started for his horse, stopping momentarily to stare at the motionless body of Walt Jenkins.

"And you were so certain that I'd be the one to die early, weren't you, Walt?"

Then Jamie climbed back on his horse. Looking back at the pair of bodies on the ground, Jamie remembered that he was growing hungry.

Three warm plates of food waited for them back at the McGregor ranch. On this day, two of them would grow cold and uneaten.

As the late rancher's son rode away to dinner, one of the men on the ground briefly opened his eyes.

Then they closed again.

Chapter Seven

Once they were about twenty miles out-side of town, Malone drew rein. "This is as good a place as any to try out that gun."

"You really mean that?"

"Sure, I do, Damon. Get it out here."

Damon scrambled down from his horse. After fumbling in his saddlebags for the package, he ripped it open to reveal the gun. Gates slung the belt around his hips, buckled it into place, and tied down the leather thong around his leg.

"This, here, is quite a gun," Damon said. "You can be cer-tain, Kell, that I'll pay you back every penny for it."

"Pay me back, huh. That's a topic I want to talk to you about a little later."

As the gun hung there on his right hip, Gates made an awkward attempt at a fast draw. The gun almost fell from his hand into the dirt.

Malone smiled to himself, pleased the gun wasn't yet loaded.

"You might want these, too," Malone said, tossing him a

box full of cartridges.

Gates quickly opened the box, thumbing shells into his gun belt, and then six more into his Colt.

By this time, Malone had climbed down from his horse.

"You see that small, white rock, about fifty yards to your right?" Kell asked. "See if you can hit that."

Gates fumbled with another fast draw.

"Wait, Damon!" Kell said. "Draw the gun slowly and deliberately for now. Aim carefully. And then squeeze off your shot. Just ease back the trigger until it fires."

Damon nodded.

"But the first thing you need to keep in mind," Malone said, "is where your shot might go if you miss your target. It's hard to unfire a bullet once it leaves the barrel of your gun. Trust me, Damon. If you miss the thing at which you were aiming, you don't want to kill an innocent bystander, a child, or someone's livestock. Always be certain of your target and your backstop."

Taking his mentor's advice to heart, Damon slowly removed the gun from his holster, sighted down the barrel, and squeezed off two quick shots at the rock.

Both of them missed and, fortunately for Gates, the rock wasn't armed.

Gates muttered a quiet swear word before he aimed again, missing the rock for the third straight time. But the black man's fourth shot split the rock into dust and tiny, broken pebbles.

Malone allowed Gates to continue shooting for a while longer. And by the time the box was empty, Damon was hitting nearly twice as many shots as he was missing.

"Come on, Damon. Put that thing away," Kell said. "Let's put a few more miles behind us before nightfall."

* * * *

Kane Coleman had been doing some chores around the ranch when he first heard the rifle shots. There had been a quick pair of them. Then it had been silent for a time, followed by three more shots, which sounded like they came from a different gun.

At first, he decided to ignore them, figuring they were simply the actions of somebody hunting wild game. But it seemed unlikely that somebody would be hunting that close to his place.

The more he thought about it, the more Kane became convinced the shooting came from just down the road.

Slapping the spurs to his mount, he headed down to the road, still seeing nothing.

About that time, he spotted a saddled horse with no rider, which was snuffing around at something on the ground. As he rode closer, Coleman could see that it was a man's body.

Then he saw the second one.

Uncertain of what he'd stumbled upon, or the danger that might still exist here, Kane pulled his rifle from the scabbard and carefully scanned the hillside. Finally satisfied that whatever danger had existed earlier had already been played out on the two souls upon the ground, Coleman raced his horse towards the pair of fallen bodies.

The first body he came to was Robert McGregor, shot once in the back and another couple of times from close range. In fact, one of the shots had been so close, the wealthy rancher's clothes were smoldering slightly from the powder burns.

There was no doubt McGregor was dead.

Speaking softly to the horse sniffing at the other body, he caught up the animal's fallen reins. On the ground was the body of Walt Jenkins. He had a pair of wounds in the back, one from a rifle and another close range shot, intended to finish him off.

The person who tried to kill this pair of men failed to realize the sheer strength and hardy resolve of the long-time ranch foreman.

Walt Jenkins was still breathing.

* * * *

Later that evening, with many long miles stretched out behind them, the two riders had set up camp for the night. After eating their dinner, Malone and Gates shared some coffee and conversation.

Admiring how the firelight danced off the metal, Gates still held the gun in his hand, pointing it out toward the darkness. "Even if I learn to shoot this thing with accuracy, Kell, do you ever think I'll be fast enough?"

"Fast enough for what?"

"Fast enough to live."

"Let me tell you something, Damon. Speed's a relative thing. It can be a help to you or it can get you killed," Kell replied. "But it isn't your speed that'll determine if you can help this family, against all odds to hang onto their place. That will be determined by your heart."

"Heart?"

72

"Heart," Kell said, taking a sip of his coffee before answering further. "When those men back there tried to hang you, it was only your strength and stubborn will to survive that kept that rope from choking the life out of you. It was your heart, Damon. A lesser man wouldn't have survived that.

"But when the bullets start flying all around you, what really matters isn't speed. It's being able to make your shots count. In order to win this type of a battle, you may have to determine that, even if you take a mortal wound, you simply won't die until you live long enough to kill your attackers."

Damon smiled. "So this is another lesson, then?"

"In a sense," Kell said. "But this is the lesson you already know something about. Nobody needs to teach you about heart. I saw that when you were hanging from a tree limb. And I saw that quality displayed again when you decided to help these people keep their place. They're lucky to have you."

Damon said nothing further for a time, as he stared down at the gun in his hand. After a few minutes, he holstered the weapon.

"You said something earlier, Kell, that still has me scratching my head."

"What was that?"

"You were talking about me paying you back for the gun. I got the idea you weren't talking about money."

"Well, I was and I wasn't."

"What's that mean?"

"You still have that envelope that was sent to Burns. You could have paid for the gun out of that money."

"But the money isn't mine, Kell."

"Although I have to say that I admire your line of thinking—I even agree with it—the fact still remains, a mighty good case could be made for the idea that Burns' money belongs to anyone brave enough to come to their aid. That's you, Damon."

"Maybe so, but I still plan on returning the money to them."

"I figured as much. So that brings me back to the idea I originally had in mind."

"And what was that?"

"The country's changing, Damon. It's growing up. It needs people to grow along with it. It doesn't really matter what color your skin happens to be, a person needs an education. A man needs to know how to read and to write."

"But what's that got to do with me?"

"It has everything to do with you, Damon. You told me you couldn't read, didn't you?"

"Well, yes. But I'm much too old to learn to read now."

"A man's never too old to try to learn something new. I knew a man one time who owned a real nice farm back East," Kell said.

Malone walked over to the fire, stirred the coals, and then tossed some more wood on top of the flames. After pouring himself another cup of coffee, Kell took another taste of it and sat down to resume his story.

"This man told me that when he was younger, he always wanted some fruit trees on his place. But at the time, the man figured he probably wouldn't live long enough to pick any apples off of them. So he just let it go."

"Maybe he knew what he was talking about, Kell."

"That isn't what he thought. The man told me that sometimes late in the evening, he'd be sitting out in front of his house, staring down at the place he meant to plant those trees. Then he'd just cuss himself."

"Why was that?"

"If he'd just gone ahead and planted those trees thirty years earlier, he said he'd be there now, cutting the peeling off one right now," Kell said, before taking another drink from his cup. "None of us knows how much time we'll have, Damon. I've seen innocent kids die in childhood and evil men live until they were ninety.

"A wise man will grab every moment of life like it could end tomorrow, but prepare for life like he'll be around forever. You want me to teach you to use a gun; then I'm going to want something from you in return."

"What's that?"

"I want you to learn to read."

"But how, Kell?"

"We'll start with the letter, the letter to Burns. By the time the two of us get to the Coleman place, you'll be able to read the letter they sent him."

"Okay, Kell. I'll try."

"Good. If that letter's going to be the thing that gets you killed, you might as well know what is says."

"And if I live?"

"Then Lizzie will have one more reason to be proud of you."

* * * *

BEATRICE WAS WAITING OUTSIDE, WHEN KANE FI-nally came racing back to the house with the buckboard.

Matt was riding in the back, caring for the wounded ranch foreman.

Next to them both was the dead body of Robert McGregor.

Coming to a stop in front of the house, Kane scrambled down from his seat, hurrying around to the back.

"Glad to see you made it back," Bea said. "How's Walt doing?"

"Not very good," Kane replied. "He's lost a lot of blood."

"I've got a place fixed up and waiting for him inside the house."

"Good," Kane said. "Let's get him inside."

Kane Coleman strained to lift the foreman's body, cradling him in his arms as he began carrying him towards the house.

"Matt," Beatrice said, "you go put the buckboard away; get McGregor's worthless hide out of the sun. Then you hurry back inside, to see if there's anything else we need you to do. You hear me?"

"Yes, ma'am. I'll do it right now."

Despite her hasty instructions to her grandson, Bea still managed to race ahead of Kane and have the door pulled open for him as he approached. "Follow me, Kane," she said, leading him to her own small, bedroom in the back.

Kane could see that preparations had already been made for his return, with hot water and bandages already waiting alongside the bed.

Kane placed Walt's body down on the bed.

"Help me to roll him over, Ma, so you can get to his wounds."

As the two of them turned the man over, Bea winced as she saw the bloody pair of gunshot wounds for the first time. But like an old hand with gun injuries, Bea began stripping the bloody and tattered shirt from Jenkins' body, starting to clean the wounds in preparation for removing the bullets."

For the first time, Kane noticed his wife was nowhere to be seen.

"Ma, where's Ann?"

"When you went back for Walt, I sent her into town to fetch the doctor."

"That's probably good thinking, Ma. I'm afraid Jenkins is going to need a whole lot more doctoring than we're capable of doing."

Despite her calm and capable work on the foreman's wounds, Kane could see the deep sense of worry and fear in his mother's eyes.

"I sure hope the doc makes it in time," she said.

"So do I, ma. So do I."

Chapter Eight

Beatrice stayed close by the wounded man's bedside while Doc Stewart carefully tended to his wounds. Kane and Annibel waited in the next room.

"I don't think the man's going to make it," Kane said, as Ann poured him a cup of coffee. "Jenkins lost way too much blood."

"Bea will be devastated."

"As much as I'd hate to see her go through that pain," Kane said, "that isn't the worst of it."

"What do you mean?"

"I mean there's going to be hell to pay when the doctor gets back to town and tells everyone that Robert McGregor was murdered, right after he left my place."

"You don't think they'll blame you, do they?"

"Who else would they blame? And I know Jamie McGregor will!"

"If you meant to kill the two of them, then why would you get the doctor, Kane? It doesn't make any sense."

"It doesn't make any sense to you, or anybody who takes

the time to think. But most people don't do that, Ann. They get worked up into a frenzy to kill or get revenge; I've seen it."

"So have I. That's why I'm a Quaker."

"Even if Walt Jenkins knows who shot them, he probably won't live long enough to tell anybody. I know you don't want him here, Ann, but I hope Gabriel Burns makes it here soon. He might be our only chance."

"Our only chance to live is a hired killer," Ann said. "God help us all."

* * * *

THREE STRAIGHT SHOTS TOPPLED THREE STRAIGHT cans from their placements.

"That's much better," Kell said. "You might just learn to shoot a gun after all."

Damon forked his horse as the two of them started down the trail. "I'm still mighty slow getting into action."

"That'll get better as your shooting improves. And like I said..."

"I know! I know!" he said, not giving Malone a chance to finish. "Accuracy always trumps speed."

"I never had a chance to ask you yet. Who taught you the alphabet?"

"Some white kids back on the plantation. But I never knew what they had to do with reading until now."

"It's real hard to learn reading without them."

"Go ahead and say it, Kell. I know you've thought it. You've been wondering why Lizzie didn't teach me."

"It did cross my mind a time or two"

"She tried to, Kell, a couple of times. But there's certain things a man don't want to learn from his wife."

"Nothing wrong with that. I'm a proud man too."

"What about you? Would you let *your* wife teach you how to read?"

"Glad I never had to find out," Malone said. "The woman's taught me a lot of things, most of the time when I pretended I wasn't listening."

Damon looked off towards the distant mountain peaks. There was a beauty to them he'd never seen. He longed to know what was on the other side of those mountains, to see it with his own eyes.

"This land, Kell, really sets a man to thinking."

"I know what you mean. The more you make your bed in wild country, the more you become a part of it. And the more it becomes a part of you."

"Maybe I'll cross those mountains some day, take my Lizzie with me. I'd like to see it with my own eyes," Damon said. "They tell me there's a big, blue sea of water over there. I hear it's even bigger than the Mississippi."

"I've heard that too."

"You've never seen it for yourself, Kell?"

"Not yet."

"What's keeping you from it? It's not like anybody has you in chains."

Malone laughed without humor.

"What's so funny?"

"Damon, you aren't the only one who knows something about not having your freedom."

"How could you know anything about what it's like to

be a slave?"

"I spent seven years of my life," Kell said, "in Yuma Prison."

"I had no idea."

"No. No, you didn't."

As Malone recalled those years in prison, and the death of his first wife, it stirred all of his old feelings of loss, rage, and bitterness. Whenever he thought he'd finally put those feelings behind him, something like this would happen, or somebody would say the wrong thing, which brought all those long-buried skeletons back to the surface.

"Although I was later cleared of the charges, it didn't get those years of my life back. And it didn't bring Alice back, who died while I was locked up."

"I'm sorry to hear that, Kell."

"It's nothing akin to being born into slavery."

"No, it's worse," Damon said. "Back then, I could only imagine what freedom might feel like. You'd experienced it; you'd lived it. Then it was taken away, through no fault of your own. Now that I've finally gotten to know how good freedom tastes, I can't imagine ever giving it up."

They continued riding Westward, neither of them speaking for a time, content to change the subject. They were also happy to let the wilderness speak to them in a way that only she could. Damon had only recently learned to hear and appreciate her voice.

"It's probably none of my business," Damon said. "But I noticed that you picked up a telegram in that last town we came to. You've not said anything about it. Is everything all right at home?"

"Sure," Kell said, "everything is fine. Rachel just told me that she's going to have a child. I'm just feeling a little guilty about being away right now. This will be my second child, the first one since Rachel and I got married."

"Congratulations, Kell. My Lizzie and I could never have children. Always felt that I missed out on something special."

"You are right about that. Jesse, my son from my first wife, is one of the best things that ever happened to me."

"Do you ever think of her much? Alice, I mean?"

"Not as much as before, but probably more than I should. I'll be sitting by myself sometimes, staring off towards the horizon. Rachel pretends she doesn't notice, but I know she does. And I think she's probably a little jealous of someone she's never even met.

"Along with that, I'm also a little afraid they'll come a day when I won't remember. With each passing year, it gets harder to recall certain details. Then I feel guilty for going on with my life without her."

"Sometimes," Damon said, "it seems like the pleasant memories, the ones you want to hang on to, are always the first ones to fade."

"I guess so."

"Don't you think Alice would want you to go on with your life?"

"I suppose."

"Very few men ever experience true love, sharing their life with one special woman, like my Lizzie, who gives up everything for them. When you lost yours, life saw fit to give you a second chance. You are truly a lucky man, Kellen Malone."

* * * *

WHILE DRYING HIS HANDS ON A TOWEL, BEA AND the doctor came out of the room.

"Is Jenkins going to make it, Doc?"

"I just don't know, Kane," he said. "Wish I had a better answer for you, but I don't. I've done everything that I know to do. It's up to God now. And him."

"Can I get you anything, doctor?"

"No, thanks," he said. "I really need to check on Mrs. Price before I get back to town. She could have that baby just about any time."

"Be sure and tell her we're thinking about her," Ann said.

"You can count on it," he said, while rolling down his sleeves and putting back on his coat. "Kane, do you want me to take Robert's body back to town? I can just take your buckboard and you can pick it up tomorrow."

"I'd be much obliged, Doc."

"What do you want me to say?"

"Don't know what you can say. I found their bodies only right after someone drygulched them. It isn't much of an explanation, I know, but it's the truth."

"You think that explanation will satisfy, Jamie McGregor?"

Kane merely laughed.

"Who do you suppose did it?"

"I've got no idea, Doc. McGregor just got done telling us that we were free to stay here, without any interference from him. Now...now we've got nothing."

"Listen, Kane, Ann, as sorry as I'd be to see you go, I think you should consider packing up your things and getting out of here right now, before anyone knows about McGregor. You need to leave; you need to go tonight."

"But everything I have's right here," Kane said.

"Not everything. You still have your lives."

"I just can't, Doc."

"You know Jamie McGregor. You know him like I do. He's crazy. And if he thinks you had anything to do with killing his father, then there's nothing he won't do to get revenge."

Kane reached out and shook the doctor's hand. "I'm sorry, Doc. Not that I don't appreciate what you're trying to do, but my mind's made up. We're staying."

The doctor reached for the door handle as he put on his hat. "Okay, then. I've done my best. With you being a Quaker, Ann, I know how you deplore violence. Maybe you can talk some sense into him."

"You're right, Doctor. I am a Quaker and I do hate violence. But I also love my husband. As misguided as I think his decision might yet prove to be, you should also know that this Quaker will always stand beside him."

"Remarkable," Doc Stewart said, as he went out the door.

* * * *

WITH HIS CHAIR TIPPED BACK ON TWO LEGS AND his boots crossed, one on top of the other on his desk, Sheriff Miles Milborn was sound asleep. Interrupted in mid-snore by the door being thrown open, the sheriff almost tumbled backwards onto the floor.

The aged lawman grabbed for his gun but came up empty-handed, the weapon already crashing from his holster to the floor in the midst of the excitement.

"What's the meaning of this?" he said, stopping only when he saw the face of his visitor. "Oh, it's you, Mr. McGregor."

Jamie McGregor was not alone. Flanking him were a couple of the hands from the ranch, ones who specialized in skills other than roping and branding.

"Yes, it's me. Who did you think it'd be this time of morning?"

"I just thought it might be..." the sheriff said. "Never mind. What can I do for you?"

"My pa is dead, Miles. What do you plan to do about it?"

"I figured I'd make a trip out to the scene later. Maybe I could pick up some clues as to the killer."

"Clues? What do you need with clues, Sheriff? We all know who the killer is. It's that sodbuster, Kane Coleman. Why don't you just go out and arrest him?"

"With what evidence?"

"You go arrest the man and I'll get you some evidence."

"I might be getting a little old and forgetful, Jamie, but I do remember that's not exactly how it works. And since your father was responsible for me getting this job, you can bet I have every reason to want to see his killer punished too."

"Good. That's more like it. When do we go?"

"We're not going anywhere, Jamie. You're staying in town or on your ranch until I know something more. And when I do, I promise you'll be the first one to know." Miles touched the young man on the shoulders, trying to direct him towards the door. Jamie shook the sheriff's hand aside. "Now go on back home and wait until you hear from me."

"Okay, I'll go, for now," Jamie said. "But don't wait too long before you do something, or I'll be forced to handle the matter myself. Coleman and his family have already killed four of our people."

"Four?"

"Yes, four. Yancy, Scarborough, Pa, and Jenkins."

"But Walt's not dead yet. Or he wasn't dead when the doctor left the Coleman place last night."

"Where's he at now?"

"Far as I know, Walt's still out to the Coleman place."

"You mean you left him there with those killers?"

"Coleman said he didn't do it, Jamie."

"And you believe him?"

"Don't know any reason why I shouldn't."

"But what if Jenkins saw the killer, Miles? He's the only person alive who can tell us who did it. I'll send some of my people over there to get him. Besides, we can take better care of him back at the ranch."

"You can't do that, Jamie. According to Doc Stewart, Walt's too injured to move right now. If you move him, you'll kill him."

"I'd still feel better if Jenkins was away from those people."

"If Walt saw something, I reckon he'll tell us when he's able."

"But what if Coleman kills him first?"

"But, Jamie, why would he do that?"

"So Jenkins can't point him out as the killer."

"Okay, Jamie, I know I'm not very smart. Now let me see if I get this. Your father and Walt ride out to the Coleman place to tell Kane he'll allow them to stay on McGregor range."

"Let Coleman stay on Pa's land? Where'd you hear that?"

"I got that from Doc Stewart, who got it from Kane Coleman."

"Well that's *his* version of the story."

"Okay, Jamie. It doesn't really matter what they talked about now, does it? After your pa and Walt leave his place, Kane follows them. Then he shoots down the pair of them on the road back home. But he only kills one of them.

"So instead of killing the only other man who knows about your father's murder, Kane takes him back to his place and calls the doctor to patch him up," Miles said. "That doesn't make much sense, does it?"

"Maybe he just did it to remove suspicion from himself."

"And risk a hangman's rope if Walt talks? Coleman would be a fool if he didn't finish him off right there on the road. I would have."

"It doesn't really matter what you think. I still believe Coleman and his family are guilty of this murder and the others."

"Then let me give you a word of friendly advice."

"What's that?"

"If they're the ones that done it, Jamie, and you keep going after them, maybe you'd better get busy hiring yourself some more help."

Jamie said nothing further, stomping away into the street.

The sheriff stood in the doorway, watching the young man and his two body guards walk away.

"That kid's going to be nothing but trouble," Miles said

to himself, resting his hand on an empty holster. "I suppose I'd better find my shooter before getting a posse together."

Chapter Nine

"Looks like we might be around here a few days," Malone said. "I'm going over to the hotel and see if they have a room for us."

"What do you want me to do?"

"You go over to the sheriff's office, Damon. Good a place as any to find out the way to the Coleman place."

"Okay, boss. What then?"

"As soon as you've talked to the sheriff, come and meet me at the saloon. Then we'll figure out what our next play is. And, Damon."

"What's that?"

"Stop calling me boss."

* * * *

"Blood all over the ground?" said the half-white, half-Yacqui tracker, Santee. "Two men were shot here, sheriff."

"It had to come from there," Miles said. "On that hilltop. That's the only place the killer could keep from being spotted and still fully cover the road." The sheriff removed his hat and mopped his brow with a handkerchief. "I'm going up there and look around. You and the other men fan out. See if you can pick up any sign."

"Yes, sheriff."

The tracker simply stood there, like he was waiting for further instructions.

"Is there something else you need?" Miles said.

"Coleman tells the truth."

"Why do you say that?"

"Two horse prints belong to Jenkins and McGregor. Over there is the print of Coleman's horse while he is riding," he added. "Coleman squats next to them here. And over there, he puts them on wagon. One other set of prints. Ridden by a white man."

Inwardly, Milborn wondered how Santee could possibly know the skin color of an unknown, mounted man on horseback. But based on past experience, Miles knew better than to second-guess the tracker's insights.

And even had those thoughts crossed his mind, the sheriff would've been fearful of voicing them out loud. Milborn was about half scared of Santee. The Yacqui half.

"Is there anything else, Santee?"

"That is all I speak, sheriff."

Milborn often suspected the tracker's careful study of the signs revealed much more than Santee would ever say. On this day, the sheriff had the same feeling.

"Okay, Santee. You and the others keep looking. See if you can find anything else. If you need me, I'll be...oh hell, you can find me."

The sheriff started his horse up on the hilltop to scout the area where the killer had waited. Milborn already had a suspicion of what he might find up there.

Dropping the reins, Miles squatted down and studied the signs around him. The quiet, unassuming sheriff never approached Santee's equal as a tracker, but he could read a lot more into the signs than anybody imagined.

He could see where the man waited for several hours, marked by several cigarette stubs left by the shooter. The sheriff could tell he grew impatient after a time, sometimes tapping the toe of his boot to pass the time. He also saw where the killer had placed his rifle butt on the ground, leaning it against a large, sun-bleached rock.

Then Miles saw the one thing he feared and suspected he'd find, the hoof print of the killer's horse, along with a perfect print of the killer's boot.

It was someone known to him.

Upon seeing the pair of prints, Miles was sure Santee already knew the information that he'd just discovered there. He silently cursed the tracker, the half-Yacqui part of Santee that chose to keep that information to himself.

He knew Santee. The man wouldn't talk.

But he wondered how much he should say, if anything. The truth of what happened here wouldn't come from Santee, but it would come out eventually.

* * * *

Hoping to wash away the blood stains, Coleman scooped up a couple of buckets of water from a nearby horse trough. After tossing the water on the boards in the back of the buckboard, he returned the bucket to its place outside the office.

Satisfied he'd done all he could do to clean up, Kane hitched his horse to the buggy, and climbed up into the seat.

"Where are you going, Coleman?" said the voice of one of McGregor's ranch hands, Nate Fitzsimmons. "Maybe you'd like to share a drink with us."

"I don't think so."

"Are you too good to drink with me, sodbuster?" he said, stepping in front of the buckboard.

"No. Just too busy," Coleman said. "If you'll just move aside, I'll be on my way."

"Let the man go, Fitz. Besides, you're scaring him," said Big Joe Larsen. "Grandma's the only one in *his* house who'll take on a man face-to-face. Coleman and his wife like to shoot their people in the back. The sodbuster's not used to facing a man who's looking at him."

"I am."

Larsen spun around on his heel to confront the intruder.

The man known as Big Joe was used to looking down on most of the people who crossed his path, or on those who crossed him. Rarely would he need his gun, since many of those he faced would generally back down from someone of his size.

Not today.

Big Joe turned to face a man bigger than himself. And if he had any plans of staring down Damon Gates eye-to-eye, he would've had to lift his gaze to do it.

The thought of someone physically overpowering him made Big Joe uncomfortable, but the man's self-pride still made him confident.

"Just let the man go on about his business."

"Why, ain't you just a big buck!" Joe said. "Maybe you ought to think about getting back to your cotton field and minding your own business."

The remark earned a chuckle from his partner.

"Maybe I'll start minding my own business," Damon said, "when you let this man mind his."

After seeing Big Joe Larsen handle dozens of other men with nothing more than his bare hands, Fitzsimmons had no doubts that the big man, despite the other man's size, could handle this situation as well. With that in mind, he was contented to stand back and watch the show that he knew would soon be coming.

Gates simply smiled. "Let the man go. Now."

"Now you've gone and done it," Larsen said. "Up to now, we was just having a little good, clean fun with the man. We didn't even mind one of Abe Lincoln's boys joining in. But then you had to go and get all pushy with us."

"Look, friend, I don't want any trouble."

"You hear that, Fitz? The boy don't want no trouble."

"Please let the man go."

"Please, is it? That's right polite of him, isn't it, Fitz?"

As he spoke to his friend, Larsen wheeled around to throw a hard right hand at the black man's jaw.

Damon, who guessed the attack was coming, deflected the punch with his elbow and spun the man around in front of him. With his left arm around Larsen's throat, he stuck the barrel of his gun against the right side of the man's throat.

"Like I told you before, let the man go."

Upon seeing this, a number of the townspeople stopped to watch. Some of them ducked for cover, seeking to enter a close and convenient door of a local business. Others peered through the window at the scene that was taking place before them.

Without exception, all of them thought the black man was about to die.

"I doubt he can get the both of us, Fitz. If the buck squeezes that trigger, I want you to gun him down."

"Before or after I blast his guts all over the street?" Coleman said, while pointing a double-barrel shotgun, he'd taken from underneath the seat, at Fitz's belly.

"Now, you," Damon said, "take that gun and toss it in the back of the man's buckboard."

For a moment, Fitzsimmons refused to move, glaring at the two of them from under the brim of his hat.

"I won't forget this, Coleman. And, you mister," he said, looking at Damon, "you can be certain we'll meet again."

Damon was starting to lose his patience. "The gun, I said. Now."

Fitz walked over to the buckboard, his six-gun clattering on the boards.

"And the other one too," Coleman said, motioning at him with the shotgun. "The one you wear on your back, tucked in your belt, underneath your vest."

Nate cursed softly as he threw the other pistol in the buckboard.

"The moment you let me go, buck," Larsen said, "I'm going to tear you apart and shoot whatever's left that ain't bleeding."

94

"You want to know something?" Damon said. "I believe you mean it."

Without removing his left arm from Big Joe's throat, Damon took the barrel of his gun and slammed it alongside the man's skull. Larsen tumbled to the ground in a heap.

Then he reached down and removed the unconscious man's gun from the holster and pitched it into Coleman's buckboard.

"You, Fitz, come over here and get your friend out of the street. Doubt you can carry him, but maybe you can drag him over to the doctor's office."

Fitzsimmons just stood there.

"Get moving, mister."

"This ain't done between us," Fitz said.

"It is for today."

Fitzsimmons began the difficult task of trying to drag his friend across the street, once falling down as he tried to lift him by the shoulders.

Seeing that gunplay had been avoided, many of those in the crowd began to return to the normal activities. A few of them, doing their best to hide a smile, continued to watch Nate Fitzsimmons dragging his partner toward the doctor's office.

Satisfied the danger was over, Coleman returned the shotgun to its place underneath the seat. "Thank you, mister," he said, tipping his hat.

"My pleasure. You ought to keep them guns. You might need them later and those boys can't be trusted with them."

"Sounds like good advice." With another smile and a shake of the reins, Coleman started out of town.

Damon watched the man ride away. Then he spotted Kellen Malone, watching from just down the street. As he walked down the street towards Malone, he had at least two questions on his mind.

"How long have you been standing there?"

"I thought I told you to stay out of trouble."

"No, you told me to quit calling you boss."

"At least you managed to avoid bloodshed."

"It wasn't easy."

"I saw that," Kell said. "You do know those two guys aren't likely to forget what you did to them, don't you? "

"At least one of them already made that point to me."

"Good. Just so you remember why we're here."

"Listen, Kell. I know what we came here for. And if I have any doubts," he said with a mile-wide grin, "I can now read the letter for myself."

"Now if you could just learn to shoot," Kell said. "Did you talk to the sheriff?"

"Nobody in the office."

"The one farthest away from you," Malone said.

"What's that?"

"The smaller man."

"What in the world are you talking about, Malone?"

"Back there, in the street," Kell said. "After you learned I saw everything, you were wondering if I was going to take a hand in the fight. I was leaving the big man to you."

Kell stood there thinking for a moment, looking out over the town. While he was thinking, one of the locals ambled past them.

"Hold on for just a minute," he said.

The man pulled up. "What can I do for you?"

"My name is Malone. This is my friend, Damon Gates."

The stranger shook both of their hands. "Pleased to meet you both. I'm Abel Johnson." Then he turned to face Damon. "I wouldn't want anyone knowing I said this, but it was a good thing you did back there, Mr. Gates."

"Thanks, Abel."

"Mr. Johnson," Kell said, "you wouldn't happen to know where I might find the sheriff, would you?"

"Can't say for sure. We had a shooting yesterday. Sheriff Milborn might be out with a posse. He isn't down in his office?"

"My friend already tried there." Malone scratched his forehead. "Then let me ask you something else."

"Go ahead."

"Do you know how a person can get out to the Kane Coleman place?"

"You mean you don't know?"

"Of course I don't know," Kell said. "If I had any idea where the man lived, I probably wouldn't be bothering you right now."

"I know where he lives. I guess I just figured your black friend would know where he lives too."

"What makes you think he'd know the way there anymore than I would?"

The man started laughing.

"You really don't know, do you? If you want to find your way out to the Coleman place, you might want to follow the buckboard that left here a few minutes ago. That man you just helped, that was Kane Coleman."

Chapter Ten

Aknock sounded on the woman's door. But before answering the knock, Maggie wrapped her robe a little tighter around her unmentionables.

"Oh, it's just you," she said, upon seeing her friend, Sarah.

"Sorry to disappoint you, Maggie."

"No, it's not that," she said, forcing a smile. "Guess I was just expecting someone else."

"Who was you expecting? Another love-struck cowboy?"

"No," she said with a smile, "I was hoping it was my son."

"Are you going to the funeral?"

"Why should I?"

"You *were* his wife."

Maggie threw down the last gulp of the previous cowboy's whiskey. "Just because I was married to the man didn't make me his wife."

* * * *

After the two men went to get themselves

something to eat, they followed the buckboard's tracks out to the Coleman place.

With Malone right beside him, Damon knocked on the door.

"May I help you, gentlemen?" Ann said.

Damon quickly removed his hat as Malone did likewise. "Pleased to meet you, ma'am. My name is Damon Gates. This is my friend, Kellen Malone. I'm here to speak to Kane Coleman regarding a private business matter. Is he here?"

"I am Ann Coleman, Kane's wife," she said. "He just went out back to unhitch the buckboard. Kane should be back to the house in a few minutes. Would you two men care to come in and wait on him? Perhaps I can offer you something while you wait."

"We'd be grateful, ma'am."

"Please have a seat, there at the table," she said, placing a hot cup of coffee before each of the two men. "If you'll forgive me for being forward, Kane mentioned that a rather large, black man helped him out in town today. I couldn't help but notice that you are rather large and..."

"And rather black, ma'am. I'm not ashamed of it."

"No reason you should be," Ann said. "That didn't come out the way I meant it. Hope I didn't offend you."

"Not at all, Mrs. Coleman."

"Then you *were* the one who helped him, I take it?"

"Yes, ma'am, I was."

"Then you most certainly have my gratitude."

"Who belongs to that pair of horses outside?" Kane said, storming into the door of the house. Although he made note of the strangers, his eyes locked on those of the tall, black man. "Oh, it's you again. Guess I never got a chance to thank you proper, mister. What brings the two of you out here?"

"You did, Mr. Coleman," Damon said, reaching into his coat pocket for a stained and faded envelope. "Or this letter did."

When Kane took the envelope from his hand, he saw it was the letter and the money he sent to Gabriel Burns.

"Where did you get this?"

"It was the man's final request that I return this to you."

"What happened to him?"

"He was gunned down," Damon said, "while trying to save my life."

* * * *

"Ashes to ashes, dust to dust," the preacher said, bending down to pick up a handful of dirt, before tossing it upon the lowered casket.

Assembled around the graveside were a large crowd of mourners, some who had traveled many miles to pay their last respects. Although Robert McGregor could be a stern man and utterly ruthless in business, the wealthy rancher also had many moments of great benevolence.

As a result of low interest loans made available to them, a number of the local shopkeepers owed their survival to McGregor. And in some cases, these loans had been simply wiped off the books.

As the preacher finished, several of those in attendance greeted Jamie, expressing their sympathies for the death of his father.

Jamie shook their hands, briefly speaking to dozens of

them as he moved from person-to-person.

After most of the crowd had gone their way, Miles Milborn approached him.

The sheriff leaned in towards the son of Robert McGregor, speaking in low tones, so as not to be heard. "I know what really happened to your father."

"What is it you think you know, old man?"

"Trust me; I know."

"Now's not the time for this, Miles," he said, with a strained smile on his face.

"But we have to talk about it."

"We'll talk tomorrow. I'll come to your office."

Until nearly the final person left the graveside, Jamie continued to shake hands and speak with those who'd come. Occasionally he'd pause to wipe away a tear.

Once the crowd had all departed, Jamie stood there, arms folded, watching the men shoveling dirt on his father's casket.

Chris Cagney, one of the McGregor ranch hands walked up behind Jamie, tapping him on the shoulder. Alton Davis was with him.

"What do you want to do about the Coleman place?"

"I want the same thing Pa did," Jamie said. "I want them out of there. Now that they've killed Pa, I really don't care how you do it. Just get them off my spread."

"But what about Walt?" Cagney said. "If we attack the house, Jamie, he might be killed in the shooting."

"It can't be helped," Jamie said. "That's a risk we might have to take."

"A risk *you* have to take? It sounds to me," Alton Davis

said, "like the risk is all Walt's, not yours."

"Listen, Davis, if you don't want to be here, that road that goes out there goes both ways. But you just try finding a job anywhere within five hundred miles of here if you walk out on me."

"So, what do you want us to do, Jamie?" Cagney said.

"I want you to hit the Coleman place tomorrow. Take about a dozen men." Jamie's lips upturned in a smile as the workers tamped down the last of the dirt over his father's grave. "Burn them out if you have to, Cagney. But by this time tomorrow, I want those nesters gone or I want them dead."

* * * *

"Like I said before, friend, it's not that I'm not grateful for what you did back in town. I am. It's just that I don't want somebody like you working for me."

"Somebody like me?" Damon said. "What's that mean?"

"A slave, a former slave. Might even be a runaway too."

"Kane!" Ann said, "I'm ashamed of you."

"Yes, I'm a runaway. What difference does that make, Mr. Coleman?"

"It makes a lot of difference to me."

Throughout the conversation, Malone determined he wouldn't take cards in someone else's game. Coming here was Damon's idea; it was his fight. But this latest comment by Coleman made Kell want to pull up another chair to the poker table.

Gates jumped up from his chair and started for the door. "Come on, Kell. Let's get out of here."

Malone was right on his heels.

Gates reached into his pocket and removed the letter Coleman had sent to Gabriel Burns. He flung the envelope onto the table.

"Your money's all there," Gates said. "But you might want to count it. After all, I *am* a slave and a runaway."

Ann stuck out her hand to hold them back. "Please, gentlemen, wait! Please."

Malone was all in favor of slamming the door behind them and not looking back. Gates was hesitant to leave, persuaded by the woman's heartfelt appeal.

"Kane, why are you acting this way?" Ann said. "This man, these men, they came all this way to help you. They've already helped you. And there's no good reason why they should. How can you turn down their help simply because of this man's skin color?"

"I have my reasons. And besides, Ann, I'm not turning down Malone's help. It's Gates I don't want."

"I've heard just about enough of this," Malone said. "My friend came all this way to help you. And he's the one who talked me into coming. It's only out of respect for your wife that I don't take you apart right now."

"Nobody talks to me that way in my own home! I know you're good with a gun, Malone," Coleman said, while rolling up his sleeves. "But you're about to get the whipping of your life, with my bare hands."

He rushed forward as Malone moved to meet his attack. Ann bravely stepped between them.

"Stop it, Kane! Please stop it, Mr. Malone!"

"All of you stop it!" Beatrice said, coming from her duties

in the back bedroom. Tears stained her eyes. "We have a man back there fighting for his life and all of you are fighting like children. Now take it outside or you'll answer to me, all of you."

"You heard the woman," Kane said. "Get out of my place. Get out now."

"I wasn't only talking to them, Kane Coleman. I was talking to you too."

It had been a long time since Coleman's mother scolded him like this, but those many years as a child in her household had conditioned Kane to obey her voice.

"I am sorry," Malone said, tipping his hat to the two women. "We will leave now. Come on, Damon."

"Sorry, ladies," Damon said. "I meant no harm to you, to any of you. I just wanted to help."

"I am sorry too," Ann said. "Thanks for your concern."

Kane picked up the envelope, opened it, and peeled off a couple bills. He ignored Gates, holding the money out to Malone. "Here's something for your troubles. Don't ever let it be said I'm not a reasonable man."

Malone stared blankly at the money in the man's hand. And when he lifted his gaze, there was nothing but contempt in his eyes for the one who held it.

"Keep your money. Come on, Damon. Let's ride."

"I'm with you, Kell."

"Here. I mean it," Coleman said. "Go ahead. Take the money."

"Give it to your wife," Damon said. "She might just need it to buy you a coffin."

The door slammed behind them.

As the two men forked their saddles, the door opened once again.

"I am truly sorry," Ann said, "that you came all this way for nothing, gentlemen. Please accept my sincere apology for my husband's behavior. I'm sure you wouldn't know it from your conversation, but Kane's not usually like that. He's truly a good man. I've just never seen him act this way before."

"I'm sorry too," Damon said.

"Trust me, ma'am," Kell added. "I've seen more than my share of scrapes over the years. And I think trouble is headed your way. With two women and a child counting on him, I sure hope your man knows what he's doing."

The two men said nothing further, tipping their hats, and putting their horses into a gallop down the trail towards town.

Annibel watched them disappear over the horizon.

"So do I," she said.

* * * *

Maggie stood beside the window, looking outside at the distant horizon, while the red-headed cowboy finished pulling on his boots. She scarcely even noticed the money he left on her nightstand.

"Maybe I'll come see you next time I get paid. Would you like that?"

"Be mad if you didn't."

Maggie McGregor hated this life.

It wasn't so much that she hated being a prostitute. She hated being a prostitute in the West.

Soon after marrying her, Robert McGregor had taken Maggie away from her comfortable, beloved home in Virginia.

Maggie hated this life. She hated this land. And by extension, she also hated her husband, who was now dead.

The conception of their son upon their wedding night hadn't been a gentle act of love. It was more like the culmination of a business arrangement, carried out with all the tenderness of a bull's castration.

After the birth of the child, he quickly grew cold to her.

Although Robert brought her here and left her to stay, it was firmly understood by everyone that, although they were free to use her, Maggie belonged solely to him.

All that was missing from her life was the McGregor brand, burned upon her hindquarters like hot iron on a new calf. There should be no mistaking his intentions. Robert McGregor was clearly the boss of his ranch. And Maggie was simply another heifer in his herd.

At the sound of his knock, she threw open the door.

"Jamie," she said.

"Hello, ma."

"I was hoping you'd come."

CHAPTER ELEVEN

"I WANT YOU BACK AT THE RANCH, MA. AND NOW that pa's dead, there's no reason why you can't come home."

"It's not home to me," Maggie said. "And even if I choose to move out there, it will never be home for me."

"But don't you see? You won't have to do this anymore. With pa dead, you're rich. The house, the ranch, the stock, the money, all of it belongs to you now. You can be respectable again."

Maggie slapped Jamie across the mouth. "How dare you say that to me! I'm just as respectable working here as I ever was serving your hateful father."

"I'm sorry, ma," he said, wrapping his arms around her. "I really didn't mean anything by what I said."

"I know that and I'm sorry," she said. "Will you please forgive me?"

"I already have."

"If I do this, Jamie, there's one thing I want you to know."

"And that is?"

"None of Robert McGregor's wealth means anything to

me. The only good thing he left me is you. I'll move back out to the ranch, but only because of you. Should you ever decide to leave, then I'll sell Robert's *precious* ranch and move back to Virginia."

Jamie wrapped his arms around his mother and pulled her close. "I don't care why you do it. All I know is that I want you out of this place today. I'll send a couple of the boys over to get your things and move you out there."

"Can I ask you one more thing?"

"Sure! Anything for you, ma."

"Just don't put me in the same room where your father slept."

"I can do that."

Maggie stared out the window, looking at nothing in particular. "You probably don't remember how he used to beat me, do you?"

"Beat you?" Jamie said. "For what?"

"I don't know. It was probably for being a woman. Maybe for being alive. I'm not even sure if Robert knew why he did it."

A knock sounded on the door.

Jamie answered it, shoving the barrel of his six-gun into the throat of a drunken, dim-witted cowboy.

"I'm looking for Maggie," he said.

"You must have found the wrong room, friend," he said, earing back the hammer on his revolver.

Once the man was gone, Maggie asked him the question that had been lingering on her mind since learning of Robert's death. "Did you kill him, Jamie?"

"Does it matter?"

"Not to me, but it might to the law."

* * * *

Uncertain what to do with the truth about Robert McGregor's death, Miles Milborn puzzled over the matter from his desk.

He knew he'd never been much of a sheriff. Many were the times he looked the other way at Robert McGregor's deeds, some of which might have been questionable in the eyes of the law. Despite that fact, he'd never looked the other way at something like this.

There was no question in his mind that Jamie McGregor murdered his own father. The evidence couldn't be disputed.

He wondered what Jamie wished to say to him about his father's death. What could he say about a cold-blooded murder?

He walked over to the window, staring outside at the townspeople as they went about their daily activities. Yet while looking at the ones outside, Miles saw his own image reflected in the window glass inside. It was then he saw the badge hanging upon his chest.

Miles determined that, this time, it would be different. This time, he would finally uphold the shining symbol he wore over his heart.

Pulling on his hat, he started out the door.

He remembered the pair of strangers who'd just come into town. Although he'd never met this Kellen Malone, he knew the man not only had the reputation of a gunman; he'd also been a lawman as well.

Maybe Malone will know what I should do.

The sheriff smiled as he saw the strangers' horses still tied to the hitching rail outside the diner.

Good, he thought. *They're still here.*

As a pair of men walked out of the diner, Miles could see one of them was a large black man. The other gentleman was tall and lean, wearing a matched pair of six-guns.

That has to be Kellen Malone.

"Mr. Malone," he shouted after them. "May I speak with you?"

Malone simply smiled. "Sure," he said, walking towards the sheriff, with Damon Gates right at his side.

"I'm Sheriff Miles Milborn," he said, thrusting out a hand. "Are you Kellen Malone?"

Malone shook the man's hand. "I'm Malone," he said. "This is Damon Gates. What can I do for you?"

"Pleased to meet you, Mr. Gates," Miles said, before turning back towards Malone. "Is true you once were a lawman?"

"I've done more than my share of it. Why are you asking, sheriff?"

Closely followed by the sound of a rifle blast, the whiff of a bullet struck Milborn only inches from his heart, leaving whatever else he meant to say unsaid.

Malone grabbed the wounded sheriff, gently easing his body to the ground. With Malone kneeling and Gates standing, the two of them palmed their guns, scanning all around them, trying to locate the sniper's position.

"Damon," Kell said, "go find this man a doctor."

"Don't bother," said the sheriff, wiping away the frothy blood coming from his lips. "It won't do any good."

Gates looked at the crowd that was now forming around them. "Did anybody see where that shot came from?"

One of the people pointed and said, "I think it came from down there."

With his gun still drawn, Gates looked at Malone and said, "I'm going to go check this out. Be right back."

"You be careful, Damon. I'm going to stay with him."

"Okay, Kell."

While still kneeling next to the man, Malone leaned closer to him and said. "What's this all about, sheriff?"

"Kane Coleman," he said, weakly.

"What about Coleman?" Malone said.

"He'll need your help."

Those were the man's final words.

As Malone rose from his place there on the ground, he ordered several of the men to get the sheriff's body out of the street.

Turning on his heels, Malone came face-to-face with a man who appeared to be half-white and half-Indian.

"I am Santee," he said.

* * * *

THE ATTACK ON KANE COLEMAN'S PLACE WAS swift, unexpected, and devastating.

It was a peaceful, bright, and sunny day. Floating in the sky were the big, white, cotton-like clouds, which rarely bring the promise of any rain.

Yelping and shooting, about a dozen men on horseback swarmed down upon the meager farm.

Annibel, who was removing her clean laundry from the

clothesline, was the first one to see them coming.

"Kane," she shouted. "Look!"

"Get to the house, Ann. I'll cover you," Kane said, leveling his rifle at the rider bearing down upon his wife. The rifle blast emptied the saddle, staining the man's chestnut horse the color of crimson. "Take Matt and get inside. Now!"

As reluctance soon gave way to duty, Ann tossed aside her basket of clean clothes. Scooping up the son who was nearly the same size as her, Ann sprinted towards the safety of the house.

Bullets were kicking dirt all around the two of them.

It was only when the heavy, wooden door was slammed behind them that Ann noticed the pair of bullet holes in her dress, bullet holes that came without injury.

The woman had no time to think about it, with her child still in danger. Ann ordered Matt to get down on the floor. Then she tipped the table over on its side, leaving it as shield between her son and the windows.

Startled by a sudden muzzle blast from inside the house, Ann saw that her mother-in-law had already abandoned the ailing ranch foreman and was now firing a shotgun out the window at their attackers.

Beatrice coolly squeezed the trigger, felt the harsh recoil of the gun, and asked about her son.

"He's still outside in the barn," Ann replied. "Kane's trapped. He shot one of those poor souls. The man was nearly on top of us."

"Ann, that *poor* soul," Beatrice said, "was just trying to kill you."

"It still doesn't mean someone shouldn't grieve for his

departed soul."

"Then leave it to his mother," Beatrice said, firing off another shot. "That's one soul the devil's already claimed for his own."

Beatrice ducked for cover only a moment before a bullet shattered the window glass, next to where she'd just been firing. It rained shards and broken pieces of glass all across the room.

"That was a close one," Bea said. "Do you want a gun, Annibel, or does the Quaker part of you just want to reload the one I'm shooting?"

"My husband's still out there alone. This Quaker wants a rifle."

"Well, glory be!" Bea said. "There's hope for you yet, gal."

"I want to help too, Ma."

"No, Matt. You stay down back there."

Beatrice said, "Not so fast, Ann. The boy can stay under cover and help us reload." Making sure to stay crouched beneath the gunfire, she crawled back to her grandson with a couple full boxes of shells. "You do remember how Kane taught you to do this, don't you, Matt?"

"Yes, ma'am, I do."

"That's my boy!" she said. "Just stay down back here. We'll slide the guns to you and you can slide the full ones back."

"You got it, Grandma."

"I may still be a Quaker," Ann said, squeezing off a shot at one of the riders, "but I wish Kane hadn't sent those two men away."

Beatrice glanced back at her daughter-in-law and smiled.

"I know we've had our differences over the years, Annibel, but at this moment, I've never been prouder of the wife my son chose to marry!"

"Thank you...Mom."

"Oh, my gosh, Annibel," she said. "Look! They've fired the barn. "

"And Kane's still in there!"

* * * *

Staying close to the sides of the buildings for cover, Damon made his way down the side street. He figured the shooter was already long gone. But despite his lack of experience with a revolver, Damon knew a good vantage point clearly favored the man with the long gun.

When he was almost ready to give up his search, Damon thought he heard a faint sound coming from somewhere down the street.

Following the noise, he saw a man with a rifle, attempting to force his way into a locked doorway.

The shooter's back was to him, with the rifle pointed downward. Gates saw the man's shoulders tense when he spoke.

"You, with the gun, drop it!"

The man who murdered the sheriff never hesitated. Swinging his rifle around as he brought the gun level, he managed to get off a fast but errant shot before Gates could return his fire.

Damon's one shot failed to miss.

The slug from the former slave's gun tore an ugly path through the man's chest, sending his soon-lifeless body tum-

114

bling into the dirt.

Moving slowly, with his gun still at the ready, Damon approached him like a wounded animal taken while hunting. Checking his body for any signs of life, he poked at the fallen body with his boot toe.

None of his caution was necessary.

The man was already dead.

Throughout the chase, Damon's heart had been racing like nothing he'd known in many years. He'd not felt this strange combination of fear, tension, and urgency since executing his escape from the plantation. But upon seeing the man dead, killed with his own gun, Damon felt nothing but sickness.

He walked away from the body, leaned against the building, and emptied his recent breakfast there upon the ground.

For only a moment, Damon stared at the gun he held in his hand. He noticed the once-beautiful revolver had somehow lost most of its luster. He briefly considered tossing it down into the dusty street. Then, after struggling with a dozen different emotions that tugged at his insides, he finally holstered the gun.

When Damon turned around, he looked into the eyes of Kellen Malone, who'd been followed down the street by a number of curious townspeople.

"You never told me it would be like this, Kell."

"I suppose this will be one of your final lessons," Malone said, "something I can't teach you."

"And what's that?"

"How you learn to live with the results."

* * * *

FROM HIS SPOT INSIDE THE BARN, KANE WAS HOLD-ing his own against the men from McGregor's ranch.

From the looks of the outlaws, he guessed that only a couple of them were professional gunmen. Kane thought it likely the rest of them were just simple trail hands.

Although he wasn't a very good shot, Kane had managed to kill the one who'd been riding down upon his wife. However, as little more than a man of plowshares and pruning hooks, his shooting wasn't good enough to break the force of the attack.

At best, the guns of the Coleman household had only killed one of the attackers and possibly wounded two more.

Quickly checking his gun, Kane could see that his ammunition was running thin. For the smallest moment, he toyed with the idea of making a quick dash for the house, but he knew he'd never make it alive. Also, he figured his presence in the house would allow McGregor's men to concentrate their attacks on just one place.

The only good and sound decision was to stay in the safety of the building.

Spitting out a silent oath, Kane began to rethink the wisdom of his strategy when he saw the flames licking at the side of the barn.

* * * *

FROM HER PLACE AT THE WINDOW, ANN COULD SEE a pair of McGregor's ranch hands lurking just outside the door of the burning barn. She knew there was no way she could hit them from this distance.

A more than competent rifle shot, Ann knew she could've hit them if given the chance to line up a careful shot. But every time she tried, a gunman would ride past, snapping off another quick shot at the window.

The last one scarcely missed her.

With the flames growing higher, she knew Kane would soon have to flee the burning structure. She also realized the men would simply wait, gunning down her husband when he did.

Ann feared she could do nothing for Kane, nothing but pray.

* * * *

FROM HIS SPOT INSIDE THE BARN, KANE COULD SEE his choices were growing limited. And if he stayed here, his time would be indeed short.

Kane knew McGregor's men had set fire to the barn, with the intention to not only flush him out, but also to kill the livestock that he kept inside.

Despite the fear that was building inside him, Kane determined that he wouldn't allow his animals to perish in those flames. He knew he must drive them outside.

Outside.

Quickly formulating a plan, Kane realized the animals' salvation might just be the key to his own.

Firing one more shot at one of the outlaw riders used up the final cartridge from his rifle. He fumbled in his pocket for some more.

"Only two cartridges," he said. "That might be enough to

start the ball rolling."

Coleman moved from pen-to-pen, opening the gates to free the horses and other stock from the now-blazing inferno.

Many years ago, an old Spanish gentleman told him about a strange custom they had in the Old Country. He called it "the running of the bulls."

Kane didn't remember much about it, except for the fact that it sounded like a darn good way to get yourself killed.

But in his case, Coleman was hoping his version of the event might actually save *his* life.

Whispering a quiet prayer to his wife's Quaker god, he fired two quick shots into the air in an effort to stampede the stock.

The fire-crazed animals raced out of the barn, with Kane running among the herd. Sprinting towards the house while using the animals for cover, Kane feared he would stumble and go down.

Then he saw a pair of men, riding and shooting, charging their horses right into the midst of the running animals.

One of the men was Kellen Malone, firing much faster than Kane thought any one man could trigger a pair of six-guns. Kane saw at least two of McGregor's men fall at the gunman's hand.

Looking up, Kane swallowed hard as he saw the huge, runaway slave on horseback. Damon simply smiled, his strong, black arm reaching down to him.

Kane's eyes met those of the slave and held there.

Although this strong, but stubborn man, was more than willing to die for his deeply-held sense of reckless pride, Kane was suddenly grateful that their arrival might prevent his own family from dying for it as well.

Catching hold of Damon's arm, the former slave pulled the man up onto the horse behind him. Damon spurred the horse and they were racing away.

* * * *

FROM HER PLACE THERE AT THE WINDOW, ANN FELT absolutely helpless to do anything for her husband. She whispered a quiet prayer, which was all she could think to do.

"Annibel, look at that!" her mother-in-law shouted. "Aren't those the two men who were here yesterday?"

Ann looked up from her prayer, seeing a pair of horses racing towards the house. Malone was firing his guns above the heads of the pitching horses and frightened cattle.

"Why, yes it is," she said.

"Here they come," Beatrice said.

"And Mr. Gates has Kane with him."

"Okay, Quaker lady," her mother-in-law said. "Let's say you start working that rifle and give them some covering fire."

"You try and stop me, Bea."

Chapter Twelve

As Kane and the others approached the house, one of McGregor's men rose up from his place next to the house.

Crim was a small man with darting eyes and a large bore rifle.

Malone threw a shot his way, but his horse, dodging its way through the frightened stock caused him to miss.

Ignoring the shot that scarcely missed his left shoulder, Crim leveled his rifle at the pair of men, who were sharing the same horse. He smiled to himself, figuring to get two-for-one.

But he definitely figured to kill Kane, the one man McGregor wanted dead.

* * * *

A relieved smile came to Annibel's face as she saw her husband, mounted behind the huge, black man, his horse racing towards the safety of the house.

The smile quickly faded as she saw Crim, just outside the

window, raising his gun at their horse.

Bringing the rifle to her shoulder as fast as she could, Annibel feared her shot would never come in time. Her Quaker upbringing caused her to cringe, taking aim at another living soul, whose back was all that faced her.

She squeezed the trigger at nearly the same time as Crim settled on his target.

Annibel's slug traveled the mere distance in less than a heartbeat, striking the man as his finger tensed on the trigger.

Crim left this world in a moment of shock and surprise, never facing the tear-stained eyes of the once-fervent Quaker who killed him.

But Annibel was only partly successful in keeping Crim from shooting her husband. The shot from her rifle that took Crim's life didn't keep him from getting off one of his own.

Crim's bullet tore a wicked path down the left side of the two riders, a bloody stripe marking both the black man and the one he rescued.

Damon's horse was the first one to the house. Malone's mount was only seconds behind them.

Jerking his rifle free from the scabbard, Malone dismounted before his horse came to a stop. Standing on the front steps, working the lever like shots from a Gatling gun, Malone threw down covering fire, as the other two men scrambled inside the house.

Seeing this one man alone in front of the house, one of McGregor's ranch hands thought the stranger would prove to be an easy target. Spurring his horse towards Malone, he snapped off shot after shot, smiling at the notion of his soon-to-be triumph.

A bullet struck the wooden step below Malone's boot. Another shot marked the crown of his hat. Malone simply raised his rifle, sighted down the length of the barrel, and squeezed off a shot. Then he watched the riderless animal go racing away, its stirrups slapping at the horse's sides.

After they were safely inside and seeing the brunt of the attack had been halted, Malone also backed inside the door, which Beatrice quickly slammed shut.

"Thank you, Mr. Malone," she said.

"You're quite welcome. Is everybody okay here?"

"Scared, but none the worse for wear," Bea said.

"You came back to help us again," Annibel said, after embracing her husband. "How can we ever thank you two?"

"Once again, I appreciate your help, Mr. Malone," Kane said, walking over to peer out the window. "It looks like they're gone now. I'll get Gates' money and the two of you can be on your way."

Saying nothing, Malone walked over to Kane and threw a roundhouse into his left jaw, knocking him to the floor.

"And don't you even think about getting up!" Malone said. "My patience with you is just about gone."

Despite the fact he was slow to anger, Gates had wanted to respond to Kane's remarks. But Malone had beaten him to the punch.

The former slave just stood there smiling, holding his hand over his wounded side, as a few dark trickles of blood fell to the floor from between his fingers.

"Thank you, Mr. Malone," Annibel added, glaring at her husband.

"Trust me, it was my pleasure."

"These men keep risking their lives to save you, Kane, and you pay them back by being rude to them. But that still wasn't enough for you, was it? Now you have to keep insulting them by offering money," Annibel continued, while pointing her finger down at her fallen husband. "Haven't you learned anything by now? I ought to hit you myself. These men aren't mercenaries; they're good and decent people, trying to save a bunch of strangers."

"Listen, son, I have to agree with Annibel," Beatrice said. "I know the reason you hate black people. But I lost somebody too. And you don't see me acting this way to Mr. Gates. His skin may be dark, but you can see this man's heart is just about as shiny as pure gold."

"Oh, my gosh, Kane," Annibel said. "You're bleeding."

"He's not the only one," Malone said, pointing at the wound Damon was covering with his hand. "That man you killed got off a final shot. His bullet wounded the both of them."

The woman rushed off to another room to get some water and bandages.

As Kane started to get up, he saw Malone staring at him.

"Relax, Malone. I've had enough," he said, holding up both hands in front of his chest. "You don't think too much of me, do you?"

"If I had my way, I wouldn't think of you at all." He cast a glance over at Damon. "But that man over there, the one you called a runaway slave, he seems to think your hide's worth saving. I'd like to think he's right, but you keep making it hard."

By this time, Annibel returned with clean water and

bandages. And while she worked on her husband's wound, Beatrice moved over to work on Damon.

Gates hesitated at first, but he quickly yielded, after seeing the determined look on the old woman's face.

"I didn't use to be this way," Kane explained. "What you need to know is that a runaway slave killed my father."

"Okay, I can understand that," Malone said. "A runaway slave killed your father, but it wasn't this one."

Damon looked over at the sweet woman who was cleaning and binding his wound. "Was that your husband who was killed, ma'am?"

"Yes, it was."

"Then I'm sorry."

"That was a long time ago," Beatrice said. "And besides, it didn't have anything to do with you."

"But it was done by a runaway slave, someone just like me."

"You're mistaken, sir. The man who killed my husband, and Kane's father, he wasn't the sort of man who'd risk his life for anyone else. He was an evil man. You're not anything like him, Mr. Gates."

After quickly checking out the window to make sure the riders hadn't returned, Malone could see the blaze consuming whatever was left of Coleman's barn. Even though he didn't much like the man, he hated to see anyone lose that which he worked so hard to build.

"You see that blood on the floor?" Malone said. "Both of you got shot out there, Kane. And both of you are bleeding."

"What's your point?"

"It all pretty much looks the same to me. None of this

blood's white *or* black," Malone explained. "I'd think you might have a reason to hate this man, Kane, if you could only tell me which part of this red blood on the floor belongs to Damon and which part belongs to you."

Kane hung his head.

"So what brought the two of you back here today?" Annibel said. "Cause we'd probably all be dead right now if you hadn't."

"Some Indian named Santee sent us out here," Malone said. "He said you were going to be attacked."

"The sheriff said much the same thing," Gates added, "right before he died."

Kane's head jerked around at the statement. "You saying Miles is dead?"

"Yes, he was murdered."

"How'd that happen?"

"We don't know for sure," Malone explained. "I think he might have been trying to tell us who killed Robert McGregor."

"Some folks are saying Kane did it," Beatrice said. "Or at least, that's the story I'm sure Jamie is telling everyone."

"Then who killed him?" Kane asked.

"I know the answer to that one."

At the sound of the voice, every head in the room turned. The speaker was Walt Jenkins, who was feebly holding himself up in the doorway.

"My gosh, Walt, you're wounded," Beatrice said, rushing over to help him stand. "What are you doing out of bed?"

"It's a mite hard for a man to sleep with all this shooting going on. Besides, you wanted to know who killed Robert

McGregor."

"Then who is it?" Kane asked.

Jenkins pointed at the chair and Beatrice helped him over to the table to sit down. Only after Walt picked up one of the empty cups, poured himself some coffee, and took a couple of sips, did he continue.

"He was killed by the same person who shot me. And that man was his own son, Jamie McGregor."

＊ ＊ ＊ ＊

"WHAT DO YOU MEAN YOU DIDN'T KILL HIM?" JAMIE McGregor said. "One poor farmer against a dozen of you, how could you mess that up, Nate?

"You remember Damon Gates," Fitzsimmons said, "the big black man I told you about, the one who braced me and Big Joe in town the other day?

"I remember. What about him?"

"We had Kane trapped in the barn and it was on fire. That was when this big buck, Gates, showed up. He had another guy with him, tall drink of water, looked like he knew his way around them twin guns."

At that revelation, Jamie, who was leaned back deeply into his father's well-padded desk chair with a fine cigar clenched between his teeth, suddenly leaned forward. "Twin guns, you say? Sounds like a gunman. You get his name?"

"No, we didn't."

"It doesn't matter anyway. I want you to take everybody you need out there in the morning. And you hear me now! I want you to kill them all, shoot their dead bodies full of holes, burn down their house around them, and bury the

126

ashes so deep the devil will need a shovel to find their souls."

"Yes, sir, boss. But what about Walt?"

"To hell with Walt! To hell with all of them!"

* * * *

AFTER PREPARING SOME DINNER, ANNIBEL MADE more coffee as the men took turns eating and standing guard. Beatrice was in the back room, cleaning and re-dressing the wounds on Walt Jenkins.

"Can I ask you something, Pa?" Matt Coleman said.

"Sure," Kane said, sipping a cup of coffee as he and Malone watched from the window. "You can ask me anything."

"Do you remember when you told me about how Indians and White men would both use their knives to cut open a place on their hands. And when they shook hands, it made them blood brothers. Do you remember telling me that?"

"Yes, I remember. Why are you asking?"

"According to Mr. Malone, he said the same bullet that passed through you also hit Mr. Gates first. Since the both of you swapped blood, wouldn't that sort of make the two of you blood brothers?"

"Out of the mouths of babes," Annibel said.

Damon, who was sitting at the table eating a bowl of Annibel's stew, looked over at Malone. They exchanged brief smiles, followed by stone-faced silence.

Kane scratched his head in wonder at the boy's question. Then he laughed in spite of himself. "I guess I hadn't looked at it that way. You might just might be right, son. You need to try and get some sleep now, Matt. It's been a long day for you; it's been a long day for all of us."

* * * *

As Nate Fitzsimmons and the other ranch hands prepared to start their ride to the Coleman place, Jamie McGregor joined them at the stables.

"I think I'll tag along," Jamie said, looking around for one of the other hands. "You, Peters," he said, "throw a saddle on my horse for me."

The cowhand nodded and moved to get the boss's horse.

"Be glad to have you," Nate said. "We can always use another gun."

"I need to talk to you, Jamie," Alton Davis said, "Nate's telling me you're planning another attack on Kane Coleman and his family. Is that true?"

"It is."

"Can you tell me why didn't I hear about it first? You asked me to be the acting foreman in Walt's absence and I've done that. This is a big ranch, Jamie, and it's getting harder to do my job without the men to run it."

"By this time tomorrow, Davis, you should have all the men you need."

"What about Walt? Were you able to get him yet?"

McGregor's eyes gleamed. "No, but I'm sure we'll get him today."

Davis scratched his head. "But how are you going to get Jenkins? Nate talked like you planned to wipe them all out."

Jamie removed his gun from the holster, checking to make sure it was fully loaded. Then he brought the gun level and fired two quick shots into the acting foreman's cowhide vest.

Alton's eyes were wide, disbelieving, and still as he tumbled into the dirt.

"Anybody else have any questions for me?" Jamie asked.

A couple of the men gasped, but nobody dared to speak. Peters lowered his head and said nothing as he handed the reins of the horse to Jamie.

"Good," Jamie replied. "Looks like we're going to need another ranch foreman. Tell me, Nate, how do you feel about a promotion?"

* * * *

While the others were sleeping, Malone and Kane were taking the final watch of the night. Malone topped off his almost-empty cup with some hot, fresh coffee. He lifted the pot towards Kane.

"You want some?"

"No, thanks," he said, chewing on a cold biscuit. "So, Malone, do you think they're done trying to kill us?"

"I don't think so. Best as I can tell, the only people who know for sure that Jamie McGregor killed his own father are all right here in this house." Malone peered through the broken window at the sun, which was just breaking in the sky. "If McGregor kills us, then he also kills the truth of what happened. It would all end here."

"Wish I could get Ann and my family out of here before they come."

"I thought about that too, but if they were caught out there by Jamie's men, there's no telling what he might do with them," Malone said, while checking the loads on his twin six-guns. "A man who'll kill his own pa is capable of just about anything. We'll just have to make our stand here and, for all their sakes, we'll have to win."

"Reckon you think I'm a fool, Malone, after all the help you and Gates have tried to give me."

"I did think that, but not now."

"You don't?"

"Hatred has a way of blinding people to things they normally ought to see. It's good to see you finally have your blinders off."

"Guess I owe you and your friend an apology."

"You don't owe me one. That debt's already been squared."

Kane lifted his hand to his face. "And I still have the sore jaw to prove it."

"When I said you didn't owe me an apology," Kell explained, "it doesn't mean my friend doesn't have one coming. It takes a big man to admit he was wrong. It takes and even bigger man to admit he's been as stone-brained and mule-headed as you've been."

"Tell me something, Malone. Do you always have this much trouble saying the things on your mind?" Kane smiled to himself. "If it wasn't for them twin guns you're wearing, I might think you're related to that Quaker woman I married. You sure you don't have a sister?"

It was then Kane's face turned serious. "I mean it, Malone. If we manage to live through this thing, I plan to give your friend a proper apology."

"Save your breath, Mr. Coleman," Gates said, lifting his head from off the pillow on which he'd been resting. "I heard every word you said and that's more than enough to satisfy me."

"How long you been awake?" Kane asked.

"Long enough to hear what you're saying," he replied. "Never killed a man before, not before I came here. You were right, Kell. It's hard to live with the results."

"If we've got any chance of living out this day, we're probably going to have to kill a whole lot more of them." Malone said, as he looked out the window and quickly lifted his rifle to his shoulder. "Here they come!"

CHAPTER THIRTEEN

THOSE IN THE HOUSE WHO WEREN'T ALREADY awake were soon stirred from their slumber by the crack of rifle fire.

Malone squeezed off a shot and the first rider tumbled from his saddle.

While Malone and Kane were already firing at McGregor's men, Damon grabbed his gun and scrambled to another window. In the back room, Beatrice left her doctoring of Walt and was firing a shotgun out the window at the riders.

Kane turned over the table to act as a shield for Annibel and Matt, who were waiting there to load the empty guns for the others.

One of the men carrying a flaming torch raced towards the house. The torch fell harmlessly to the ground after Bea nearly cut the man in half, when she let loose with both barrels of her shotgun.

Malone dropped a couple more riders before handing the empty rifle over to Annibel. Then he pulled his twin guns and began firing fast as he could locate his targets.

As Beatrice was thumbing a couple of more shells in her shotgun, a bullet from one of the riders burned the fleshy part of her arm.

"Bea's been hit," Walt said, causing Annibel to crouch beneath the gunfire as she rushed to the woman's aid.

Walt slung his gunbelt around his hips, picked up the fallen woman's gun, and hobbled to the window.

"I'm just fine, Annibel. It hardly nicked me."

"I'll be the one to decide that, you stubborn old woman," Annibel said. "Now you stay down here until I bandage your wound."

Walt began firing out the window, stopping only long enough to make sure Beatrice was okay. Seeing that the woman wasn't seriously injured, the ever-present smile returned to the wounded foreman's face.

"I knew I should've fired some of these guys," he said, just before blasting one of them backwards over the rump of a McGregor horse.

* * * *

UPON SEEING THE SMOKE FROM COLEMAN'S BARN rising high in the morning sky, a number of the townspeople began loading water buckets into a wagon. But the echoes of distant rifle shots told them that it was more than just a fire taking place at the home of Kane and Annibel Coleman.

Despite the numerous attempts by Jamie and some of his hands to circulate the story, almost nobody in town believed that Kane Coleman had anything to do with the killing of Robert McGregor. And the attempts to save the life of Walt

Jenkins, a witness to the murder, clearly weren't the actions of a guilty man.

About four men, mostly veterans of the war, quickly saddled their horses. Unwilling to let an innocent man die needlessly, they planned to do whatever they could to help. But before those men rode out together, the local shopkeeper made sure each one of them was equipped with a quality Winchester and a couple spare boxes of shells.

One man, armed with nothing but a shotgun and carrying the water buckets and blankets, plodded down the road in his buckboard, soon falling far behind the four mounted horseman.

* * * *

ONE OF MCGREGOR'S MEN WAS SHOT DOWN AS HE approached the house with one of the torches, dropping the flaming pole on the front porch.

"Cover me, Kell," Damon said, snatching up a blanket from one of their makeshift beds.

Before Malone could stop him, Gates was already out the front door.

Damon quickly beat out the fire with the blanket, as bullets struck the house all around him. But before he could get back into the house, he palmed his six-gun and shot the rider who was charging down upon him.

Yet he failed to notice the man, who'd crept in behind the back of the former slave. Damon wheeled around to face him. Bringing up his gun to face this newest threat, Gates swallowed hard, realizing his draw would be much too slow to spare his life.

134

Then a bullet tore through the remaining window glass, killing the lone gunman facing Damon Gates.

It came from the gun of Kane Coleman.

* * * *

Despite their early success in holding off the attack, Malone knew the superior numbers of McGregor's riders would eventually overwhelm them. And if they succeeded in setting fire to the house, then the defenders would be forced out into the open.

It was then that Malone made a decision.

Gates was the first to recognize that Malone deliberately moved away from his place at the window. "Kell, what are you doing?"

"I'm going out there."

"You're crazy. They'll kill you."

"Not if I kill them first. If I stay here," Malone explained, "they're going to set fire to this house. And there are women and a boy in here. I'm not going to stand by and let that happen."

"You want me to come with you?"

"Now, you're crazy. They'll kill you," he said, smiling as he checked his guns.

Malone removed the bar from the door. Grabbing iron with his right hand and earing back the hammer, his left pulled the door open slightly. Palming his other gun, Malone was ready to kick open the door with his boot and step outside to confront them.

As he eared back the hammer on his other gun, a loud volley of rifle fire sounded from the East. Several of McGregor's men began firing over their shoulders as they started to race their horses away in the opposite direction.

Plunging out onto the front step, Malone's twin guns blazed, taking down two more of the riders before they could flee.

Thinking the approaching riders had come to help, but still not confident of their intentions, Malone waited next to the house, guns fully drawn.

The others inside the house held their guns at the ready, waiting to see what Malone would do.

The lead man on horseback plunged his rifle into the scabbard, holding up his right hand as he came upon the fully armed man in front of the house. Hesitantly, the three others riding behind him did the same.

"We came to help Kane," he said to Malone.

"Then I'm pleased to meet you," Malone said, holstering his guns. "Your timing couldn't be much better."

"Glad we ain't too late."

"Right on time," Kane added, stepping outside the house.

"Was anybody hit?" one of the others asked.

"Ma got a slight scratch, but we're all okay."

"How's Walt Jenkins?" the leader of the group said.

"Still on the mend," Kane said, "but he'll make it."

"That's good to hear. There's a buckboard coming somewhere behind us," the man said, looking back in the direction of town. "When he gets here, maybe we can load Walt up and get him into town, closer to the doctor."

* * * *

WHILE WATCHING FROM A SAFE DISTANCE AWAY,

Jamie smiled as he watched the attack taking place on the Coleman house.

"You've got to admit, boss, those squatters are putting up a pretty good fight."

"It isn't the squatters," Jamie explained, flicking away the cigarette he'd been smoking . "It's the ones helping them. Kane and his family would already be dead if not for those strangers. But it won't be enough. I'll bet every one of them's dead inside of fifteen minutes."

"What makes you so sure?" Fitzsimmons asked.

Jamie pointed towards the house. "It's only a matter of time until one of those men with the torches put some flames to the house.

"That's what I'm waiting to see."

"Why's that?" Jamie said.

"That big man, the black guy, he braced me the other day. I'd pay good money to hear his final, dying screams as he burns."

"But what if he gets out?"

"Then I'll shoot a dozen bullet holes in whatever's left of the man."

"What about the other stranger?" Jamie said.

"You can have that one. They say he's lightning fast."

"Who is he?"

"His name's Kellen Malone, from the Arizona Territory."

"Kellen Malone? Here?"

"I'd only heard tell of him. A couple of the boys said they recognized him. Malone's the one who's with that big buck."

"Look at that," Jamie said. "One of them is outside the house."

"That's Malone!" Fitz said.

"It doesn't matter how fast he is," Jamie said with a laugh. "There's way too many of our riders surrounding the place. He can't kill them all. Yep, I'd say Malone's about to meet his Maker."

The first sounds of rifle fire coming from the East startled them. Jamie spat out some profanities as he saw the four riders headed towards the ranch. Yanking his rifle from its scabbard, Jamie sighted down the barrel of the gun, placing his sights on Kellen Malone, who was standing outside the Coleman house.

"I've got half a mind to teach the gunhand a lesson about sticking his nose in my business."

His finger tensed above the trigger.

"If you're going to shoot him, boss, you'd better make it fast! We've gotta get out of here."

"This is way too easy," Jamie said, lowering his rifle. "When I bring down the great and mighty Kellen Malone, I want him to see it coming first. Let's ride!"

CHAPTER FOURTEEN

THREE DAYS AFTER THE ATTACK ON THE COLEMAN place, a United States Marshal arrived in town to arrest Jamie for the murder of his father, Robert McGregor.

"The trial's scheduled for tomorrow," Kane said. "I sure hope the two of you will stick around until then."

Malone and Gates nodded.

Upon hearing a buckboard approaching the house, the three of them went outside to see who was coming.

The visitor was Maggie McGregor.

"Good morning, Mr. Coleman," she said with a smile. "I'm so glad I was able to catch you at home."

Malone offered his hand to the woman as she started to climb down.

"Thank you, Mr. Malone, is it?"

"Yes, that's me," he said.

Then the former prostitute smiled politely at the former slave. "And you would be Damon Gates, I take it?"

"Yes, ma'am."

"You care to come inside?" Kane asked.

"Thank you, Mr. Coleman. That would be very kind of you."

Once inside the house, Maggie looked all around at the damage done by the attack. Hundreds of bullet holes marked the walls. The broken windows on the house had been replaced with rough lumber. Annibel's china cabinet was empty, a constant reminder of the keepsakes they lost in the fight.

"Please have a seat," Annibel said. "May I offer you a cup of coffee?"

"No, thank you. But that is very kind."

Maggie sat silent for a time. There was the trace of a tear in her eye at the condition of the house and the hardship their family had faced. And as someone who'd been engaged in her shameful profession, Maggie wasn't used to considerate treatment from those in polite society.

"I can see that you suffered greatly in the recent attack on your home. For that, I am truly sorry."

Annibel nodded.

"For those of you who may not know, I am now the one in charge of Robert McGregor's holdings. As that person, I want you to know that you no longer have anything to fear from me, my son, or anybody who works for me.

"This property is all yours and we will make no further efforts to dispute that. And from this time forward, if anybody from the ranch should accost you in any way, please contact me immediately. I can assure you that person will be fired on the spot."

Still not sure if they could believe what they were hearing, and still uncertain if her appearance could be some kind of a ruse, Kellen Malone and Damon Gates stood close by as

Jamie's mother spoke. Standing beside them was Beatrice and young Matt.

"Mr. Coleman," she continued, "as a token of my sincerity, there will be an engineer coming to your place in the next few days. You give him the specifications for your barn, any size or layout you deem appropriate, and he will prepare the plans for its construction. Then, I will hire the men to rebuild it."

"That is very kind of you, Mrs. McGregor."

""I absolutely hate that name," she said with a nervous smile. "Will you please call me Maggie?"

"Thank you, Maggie."

The woman smiled briefly, an expression that was quickly followed by one of pain. "I am truly sorry for all the trouble that Robert and my son brought down upon you; make no mistake about that. But having said that, you also need to understand that Jamie is my only son. He's all I've got left.

"Because of that, I won't sit by and allow him to be hanged. I'll do everything in my power to see that he gets a rigorous defense. I trust you'll understand my position."

"As a mother, *I* certainly do," Annibel said.

"I'm glad you understand."

* * * *

IT CAME AS A SHOCK TO NOBODY THAT WALT Jenkins was the prosecution's primary witness. What did surprise people was Jamie's admission that he did indeed commit the murder. However, Jamie claimed that he had failed to recognize them and that the death of his father had been a tragic mistake.

141

Even more surprising was the identity of the defense attorney, Isaiah Mason, who was coaxed out of retirement.

Mason, one of the West's most prominent and successful attorneys, had been gone from the profession for nearly ten years. It was only through the persuasion of Maggie McGregor, a woman he often frequented, that Isaiah defended her son.

And while seeing him perform in the courtroom, most of the townspeople thought Mason had lost none of his edge.

During Jenkins' testimony, his attacks on the man were relentless.

"So, Mr. Jenkins," he said. "You've heard the testimony of the defendant, how that he heard a shot and only fired at you and Mr. McGregor in self-defense."

"Yes, I heard what Jamie said, which is probably just about the biggest yarn ever concocted."

Snickers could be heard around the room, forcing the judge to pound his gavel a couple of times to restore silence to the saloon, which now served as a make-shift courtroom.

"So you're saying you didn't hear the shot?"

"No, that isn't what I'm saying. What I'm trying to say is..."

"Judge," Mason said, cutting off Jenkins in mid-sentence, "will you instruct the witness to simply answer *only* the questions I ask?"

Judge Whit Thomas looked over at Jenkins. "You heard him. The witness will answer the questions without any elaboration."

Walt scratched his head. "Let me get this straight, Whit. When you're telling me to stop elaborating, it sounds like you're telling me to ignore the oath I just swore."

A couple of spectators laughed, followed by the slam of the judge's gavel.

"Just answer the man's questions, Walt."

"Yes, sir."

The lawyer continued. "Is it your testimony that you didn't hear the shot?"

"It's my testimony that there wasn't no shot to hear."

"Judge," Isaiah said.

"Just keep your answers short, Mr. Jenkins. 'Yes' and 'no' is all the court needs to hear."

"Well, it ain't all they need to hear, not if they want to get at the truth."

"Mr. Jenkins," the lawyer continued, "Before you and Mr. McGregor were attacked, did you hear the shot to which my client made reference?"

"No."

"Please let me get this straight. You're saying you didn't hear it?"

"Yes," Walt replied.

"Then you're testifying there was a shot, but you didn't hear it."

"No."

"Are you saying there wasn't a shot or that you didn't hear it?"

"Yes," Walt answered. "Now wait a minute. I mean no."

Before continuing his examination of the witness, Isaiah walked over to face the four citizens who made up the jury. "Yes or no, which is it, Mr. Jenkins?"

Jenkins was bewildered. He was confident there'd been

no other shots fired just before he and Robert McGregor had been ambushed, but the judge and the lawyer, both of whom were his long-time friends, wouldn't permit him to answer in such a way as to say that.

"Mr. Jenkins," Mason continued, "do you happen to know the penalties for perjury?"

"I didn't figure there were any."

Mason laughed without humor. "Are you saying that you believe a man can perjure himself in an American court of law and suffer no penalties for it?"

"Yes, that's exactly what I'm saying."

"What would ever give you that idea, Mr. Jenkins?"

"It's pretty simple, really. I figured if there were any penalties for perjury, Isaiah, then your law career would've ended over thirty years ago."

The room erupted with laughter.

"Silence in the court!" Judge Thomas bellowed, repeatedly slamming down his gavel on the oaken bar. "Silence in the court!"

Once order was finally restored in the room, Judge Thomas asked Mason if he had any further questions for the witness.

"No, your honor."

The judge looked over at the prosecutor. "You care to redirect?"

The lawyer shook his head.

"Then, Mr. Jenkins, you can step down." Removing a watch from the pocket of his robe, the judge checked the time. "Being that it's almost time for lunch, and remembering that there's always some fine apple pie for dessert at the diner,

144

I think we will break for something to eat now. Gentlemen, I'll expect you back here at one o'clock, in order to give your closing statements."

With another slam of the gavel, Thomas said, "This court is adjourned."

As the people left the courtroom, Maggie walked up behind Walt Jenkins and tapped him on the shoulder.

"Walter, may I speak to you for a minute?"

Upon seeing the woman behind him, Jenkins greeted the woman with a smile and a warm embrace. "It's good to see you again, Maggie. I understand that you're back out at the ranch."

"Yes, I am."

"I'm happy to see you're out of town."

From the first day that Robert McGregor had thrown his wife out of the house, Jenkins continued to be Maggie's only friend. Although the two of them rarely crossed paths, the ranch foreman never looked down on her, despite the fact he knew what she was doing to make a living.

"I know we've been friends for a long time, Walter. That is why I hate what it is that I've got to tell you."

Jenkins smiled. "Then go ahead and come out with it."

"Under the circumstances, with you testifying against Jamie," she said, wiping away a tear, "there's just no way I can keep you on at the ranch anymore."

"I understand."

"No, I'm not certain you do, Walter. If it was simply up to me, and Jamie wasn't involved, you'd stay on as long as you wanted. But it simply won't work with the two of you there."

"Jamie's on trial for his life, Maggie. What makes you so

certain that he's going to be there with you?"

"He will be acquitted. I simply won't consider anything else."

"I still think you need to prepare yourself for the worst."

"Let's not speak of that anymore, Walter. There's one other thing I want to say to you," Maggie said, while handing him an envelope. "I know you're a proud man. So this isn't charity. Inside that envelope you will find the sum of two thousand dollars."

"What in the world for?"

"Please don't think your dismissal was an easy decision for me. And to prove it to you, I wanted to compensate you for the many years of good and loyal service you gave to Robert and to this ranch. Half of it is for the service you gave to this ranch, the other half is for the injuries you sustained at the hands of my son."

Jenkins smiled and shook his head. "I can't take this."

"Yes, Walter, you will, or I will simply lay it down upon the bar for the next person to find. If you don't take this money, then I will never be able to live with myself for the decision I made. Please take the money, Walter. I implore you."

"There's no question, Maggie, that this kind of money will get me a fresh start. For that, I thank you."

Maggie walked on over to the bar, slipped around behind it, and found herself two glasses. Then she poured them each a shot of whiskey and handed the second glass to Jenkins.

Maggie lifted her glass in salute. "Here's to fresh starts, yours and mine," she said, before the two of them tossed down the drinks.

"I wanted to give you this earlier, but I was afraid that if

I gave it to you before your testimony, it might be construed as a bribe."

"I'd have never thought that," he said.

"But a lot of others would."

"Now that you have agreed to take my money," the woman said with a smile, "maybe I can persuade you to buy me lunch."

"But I just testified against your son in a murder trial, Maggie. How do you think that would look to people?"

"I'm a saloon gal and you're a man who just got fired from his job, meaning we aren't exactly the cream in society's milk pail. What do we care what anybody thinks?"

Chapter Fifteen

Before the lawyers could ever return for their closing arguments, a couple of workmen already started construction on the gallows for Jamie McGregor. And as the crowd gathered inside the saloon to hear the reading of the verdict, the pounding of the judge's gavel was almost lost in the din of new nails being hammered into lumber.

Seated behind the accused was his mother, Maggie McGregor, who reached up to place a comforting hand on Jamie's shoulder. The young man simply smiled and softly placed his hand upon hers.

Despite the difficulties of his case, Isaiah Mason maintained the same confident air about himself as when he often defended the accused and rarely lost a murder case.

Kellen Malone and Damon Gates, who arrived only a few moments before court resumed, found no empty chairs. They simply chose a place in the back of the room to stand and watch.

Seated near the front was Beatrice, who was the only person in the Coleman family who chose to attend the proceedings. Walt Jenkins selected an empty seat beside her. But despite giving her his best smile, the woman scarcely acknowledged his presence.

Of course Walt had no way of knowing that she was still angry about seeing him at lunch with a woman Beatrice often called "the town trollop."

"Will the defendant and his counsel please rise," Judge Thomas said, "for the reading of the verdict?"

As the head juror stood to read the verdict, Malone was certain he saw at least one of the jurors wink in the direction of the defendant's table. It also appeared that Maggie returned that gesture with a brief nod of the head.

As Malone looked around the room, it looked like nobody else had noticed the subtle exchange of signals between the two people.

"We the members of the jury, in the matter of the murder of Robert McGregor," the man said, "we the members find the defendant, not guilty."

Most of the crowd, already expecting the jury to return with a guilty verdict, were glued to their seats in stunned silence. It was several long seconds before their voices began buzzing about the verdict.

Malone simply shook his head and smiled.

"What's so funny, Kell?" Damon asked.

"The heart of a mother," he said.

As the U.S. Marshal removed the cuffs from his two wrists, Jamie pounded down his fist on the table in triumph. Then he hugged his attorney, followed by a much warmer embrace for his mother.

"Ma," he whispered, "what just happened here?"

"When it comes to those respectable members of the jury," Maggie said, in a tone that only her son could hear, "at least two of them were my best customers. It would appear that they didn't want their wives to know about their indiscretions."

"Come on, Ma. Let's go home now," he said. "Tonight, you and me, we're coming back. We'll get us the biggest steak in town, a bottle of wine, and celebrate."

"Thank you, members of the jury, for your service," the judge said, before pounding the gavel one final time. "That concludes this trial. Gentlemen, I also declare that this saloon is now open!"

Removing his robe, Judge Thomas handed it over to his nephew, a young law student who came for the reading of the verdict. "Go put that robe in my saddle bags," he said, "and tell those men outside, that unless they're building a house, then they might want to save those nails and lumber for a real hanging."

* * * *

"I still can't believe Jamie was acquitted," Kane said.

"I probably wouldn't have believed it," Malone said, "if I hadn't seen it with my own eyes."

"The town trollop probably paid off the jury," Beatrice said, "at least the ones who weren't already her customers."

"Oh, Bea," Annibel said, "that's a cruel thing to say about one of God's creatures."

"The woman's a creature, all right," Beatrice added. "But I'm not sure she's one of God's."

"One thing's for certain," Gates said, "it looks like Maggie McGregor kept her word about rebuilding your barn and leaving you folks alone. That has to be worth something. Maybe now you'll be free to make a real home here."

"Now that Jamie's been acquitted," Annibel said, "do you think Mrs. McGregor will go back on her word?"

"I don't think so," Malone said. "But I'm guessing that if you ever got on that woman's bad side, she could be a dreadful enemy. No, I don't think you should have any more trouble with the McGregors."

"So, that brings us to you," Kane said, looking over at the pair of men who were sitting at his dinner table. "What do the two of you plan to do from here?"

"Don't look at me," Malone said. "This has all been his doing from day one."

Gates looked startled when all eyes in the room turned to him. "I agree with Kell," he said. "I figured we'd spend the night in town and start out for Nicodemus in the morning. From here on out, I think your biggest problem is getting the soil ready for next year's crop."

"I was wrong about you, Damon, and I'm sorry," Kane said, sticking out his hand. "Without the two of you, my wife, my son, all of us would be dead right now. You're a good man. And that's the reason we wanted you to have this. Do you have that envelope, Ann?"

Annibel picked up the envelope from the mantle and placed it in Damon's hands. "The two of us talked about this," she said. "It's what the Lord wanted us to do. Please, take it."

Damon opened it up and realized it was the exact same letter and money they sent to Gabriel Burns.

"We sent that money to Burns to get his help. You came in his place," Kane said, once more offering his hand to the former slave. "I doubt that Burns could've done it any better."

"Burns," Damon said, "didn't have Kellen Malone riding with him."

"Take some of the money and buy your wife a nice dress," Beatrice said.

Malone nodded at Gates. "Take the money, Damon. You earned it."

"Okay, then," Gates said. "Thank you very much."

"Maybe now you can pay me for that gun I bought you."

Gates simply smiled. "Soon as I get some change."

"And thank you, Mr. Malone," Kane said, grasping the tall gunman's hand. "I don't know how we can ever repay you for all you've done."

Malone grinned. "I think I'm already a little ahead of you, Kane."

"Oh that," he said, rubbing his jaw. "Reckon I owe you more than money."

"I'd like to say I'm sorry about hitting you," Malone said, "but..."

"But you're not," Kane added.

"You got that right," Malone said with a smile. "But I can say it's been an experience getting to know you."

"Same here."

"Maybe the next time I'm around," Malone said, "you can collect on *that* one."

"You can count on it!"

Like battle-hardened soldiers who fought and suffered together during a war, Malone and Gates traded handshakes, embraces, and pleasantries with each one of those in the house.

"Thank you for giving us our lives back, gentlemen," Annibel said, with a smile and a wave. "And go with God."

Malone and Gates forked their horses and turned to ride away. As they started to ride away from the house, Gates suddenly drew back on the reins, walking his horse back towards the house.

Stopping right in front of Kane, Gates leaned down towards them on the saddle horn. "Didn't you tell me, Kane, that your father was killed by a runaway slave?

"That's what I said, all right."

Gates just smiled and nodded. "I never did tell you this, Kane, but I guess I can understand why you might've hated someone like me. Losing your daddy, things like that can make a lasting impression on a young person. Trust me, I know! Mine was murdered by a white slave master."

Saying nothing further, Gates reined his horse around and kicked his mount into an easy gallop until he caught up with Malone.

As Kane watched him ride away, he saw the former slave through new eyes.

* * * *

"So how did you pull it off?"

Maggie took a sip from her glass of wine. "With your life on the line, I just couldn't leave anything to chance, Jamie. Like I told you, of the four people on the jury, two of them were my biggest customers. I promised them my silence."

The woman paused long enough to make sure nobody

was close enough to hear them. "What you don't already know is that I purchased the verdict I needed from one of the others. There was no way you were going to hang for killing that diseased and insufferable man."

"Thank you, ma," Jamie said with a smile.

"I'll catch up with you later," he said, getting up to leave.

"Okay. See you at home."

After Jamie left the diner, Maggie lingered at the table slowly sipping her wine. For the first time in years, the woman felt good about her life. She even thought the change in circumstances might make her reconsider her hatred for the West.

With Robert gone, Maggie thought it might be possible that she would finally realize her life-long dream to have a home, a son, and a life worth the living. Motioning the waiter over to her table, she paid for their wine and dinner and anonymously picked up the costs for the other patrons.

She was smiling as she left the diner.

Approaching the buckboard for her return to the ranch, a person leaped out from the darkness and grabbed her, pulling the woman deeper into the shadows. She tried to cry out for help, but her attempts to yell were thwarted by a hand clasped firmly over her mouth.

Her attacker said nothing. The man's strong and brutal arms continued to pull her deeper into the darkness of the night, which provided safety for the actions of evil. She struggled to break free, but to no avail.

It was then he produced a knife, the glint of its blade reflected in the brightness of the moonlight. She felt the sharp edge of the blade touching her throat, clearly designed to discourage any loud cries for help.

"Please don't hurt me," she pleaded, quietly. "Whatever it is you want, I'll give it to you. I mean it, anything you want! Please, just don't kill me."

"What makes you think you have anything I want, mother?"

"Jamie!"

"Yes, mother, it's your *loving* son."

Maggie was bewildered. "Why are you doing this?"

"Surely you weren't foolish enough to think that I'd just let you, a simple whore, take over my father's vast fortune. What kind of an idiot do you think I am? You've already wasted the ranch's money by rebuilding the barn for those worthless sod busters."

"But I didn't even want this, son. I never cared about the money," Maggie said, her tears falling on her son's arm. "Everything I was doing was solely for you, Jamie. Didn't I get you acquitted for murder charges? What more proof do I need?"

"For that one thing, I thank you, but that doesn't change the facts of what you were and still are. Pa was right about you."

Maggie couldn't believe what was happening. A couple of days earlier, she'd thought about taking her own life. But now that she'd finally discovered some reasons that motivated her to live, it was all a lie. Her own son was preparing to take her life.

The woman sobbed uncontrollably.

"After you getting me freed, our touching reunion, and

the excellent meal we just enjoyed in front of all those fine people in the diner, not a one of them will ever suspect that I killed the both of you. They'll just think it was one of your drunken customers."

"If you're going to kill me, Jamie, then just get it over with."

Jamie raised the knife. "As you wish, mother. Say "hello" to daddy for me."

"You, with the knife," a voice from the shadows said, "drop it!"

CHAPTER SIXTEEN

Upon returning to town, Malone and Gates thought they would turn in for the night and get a fresh start for Nicodemus in the morning. But as Malone was about to tie his horse to the hitching rail in front of the hotel, he saw a couple of lone figures disappear into the darkness.

"Would you mind getting this, Damon?" he said, while dropping the reins. "I want to go check this out."

"You need any help?"

"No," Malone said. "I'm sure it's nothing."

"Okay, Kell. Suit yourself. I'll see you in a little bit."

After tying up their horses, the former slave threw their pair of saddle bags up over his left shoulder. Then he started up the stairs to his room. As Damon reached out to turn the door handle, he suddenly had a notion that he ought to check on Malone.

Gates turned on his heel as a couple of bullets tore through the door.

* * * *

"Drop the knife or I'll kill you," Malone said.

"Please don't shoot him, Mr. Malone."

"But he's threatening to kill you, Maggie."

"He doesn't really mean it."

"Pardon me, ma'am, but the man had a knife to your throat. Killing you is exactly what your son had in mind."

"Maybe you and the cotton picker ought to try minding your own business for a change, Malone."

"Jamie, put down the knife! I'm not going to tell you again."

"Okay, I'm going to do like you want," Jamie said, while throwing down the knife. "This is all a big misunderstanding. Tell him, ma."

"My son is right. It's a misunderstanding," Maggie said. "Please, Mr. Malone. Everything will be fine now."

"It's your decision, ma'am," Malone said, holstering his gun. "But if you don't mind, I'll just take this knife with me for safekeeping."

But as Malone started to reach down to pick up the knife, Jamie saw it as an opportunity.

McGregor's hand swept down towards his gun.

* * * *

The pair of bullets splintered the door right where Gates had just been standing. It was only his sudden decision to check on Malone that spared his life.

Damon palmed his gun as he tossed the heavy saddle-bags onto the floor, hoping to make it sound like a body had fallen there.

The ruse worked.

Big Joe Larsen, who'd been waiting in the room to kill them, threw open the door and stepped into the hallway. Despite the fact that his gun was still drawn, the smile disappeared from Joe's face as he saw Gates standing there.

Even after being taken by surprise, Larsen's gun came level in the blink of an eye. But the gun of Damon Gates was already stabbing flame.

One of Damon's bullets pierced his chest, leaving a crimson stain on the wall behind him. His second shot staggered the man, causing Joe to fire wildly.

The wayward bullet from Joe's gun tore through one of the hotel walls, barely missing a sleeping businessman.

Big Joe weakly tumbled onto on the floor, his body dying in the same place he'd meant for Gates' body to fall. Gates kicked away the revolver from his dying hand.

A voice from inside Gates' room shouted, "Please don't shoot me, mister. I'm coming out."

"If I so much as even think I smell a gun, I'll blast you full of holes," Gates said. "You understand me?"

A gun flew out the door ahead of the man.

Following the gun, there emerged a wolfish little man, ghost-white pale, holding his hands high in the air. As he stared down the dark and deadly bore of Gates' six-gun, a look of terror filled the man's eyes. "Please don't kill me, friend," he pleaded. "I'm done with guns forever."

Gates motioned with the barrel of his gun toward the hallway. "If I ever see your face again, I'll shoot you on sight. Now ride!"

The man sprinted for the stairs, forked his horse, and didn't quit riding for the next two days.

A number of the hotel's patrons, most of them still in their robes and bed clothes, came out of their rooms into the hallway. The hotel manager crept up the stairs, saw the body, and dashed back down to find the U.S. Marshal.

"They said Malone would be hard to kill, but I had no idea you'd be that good," Joe said, only seconds before his eyes closed forever.

Realizing that this attack on them had been planned as an ambush, Gates wondered about what had happened to Malone.

But upon hearing gunfire from down the street, Gates raced for the stairs.

* * * *

"Jamie, no!"

At the cry of Maggie's voice and upon the sound of gunshots up the street, Malone's left hand palmed his gun. While still bent over to pick up the knife, Malone crouched low and fired at her son.

Their two bullets crossed paths in the air, Jamie's bullet creasing the crown of Malone's hat, before it entered the backside of the saloon.

But the slug from Malone's gun was straight and true in finding its target. It struck the outlaw only inches from his heart.

"No!" Maggie screamed.

Confident in his ability to prevail in any gunfight, Jamie McGregor simply stood there in stunned disbelief. His left hand clutched at his chest, raising the bloody hand in front of his dim and staring eyes.

The gun tumbled off the end of Jamie's weakened fingers. The young man tried to speak, but no words came to his lips. Jamie swayed on his feet before he started to fall, his mother catching him before he went face-forward into the dirt.

Holstering his gun, Malone moved to help her.

"Get away from him!" Maggie said. "Get away from both of us."

The woman eased her son's dying body onto the ground, cradling his head in her lap. Maggie held him there, singing to him softly, as his life's blood marked her dress and the final moments of his life ticked away from life's indiscriminate clock.

Gun drawn, following the sound of the shooting, Gates sprinted down the street behind Malone.

Their eyes met, but neither of them spoke.

Upon seeing the scene spread out there before him, Gates felt compelled to remove his hat at the woman's loss.

With all of the shooting that was taking place in the town, a huge crowd began to gather behind them. U.S. Marshal Jim Cowdery, who'd known Malone for many years, also came down the street. Although the witnesses had already briefed Cowdery on the details of the two shootings, he still needed to confirm the facts with Malone and Gates.

Tears rolled down her cheeks as Maggie reached up to close her son's still and unseeing eyes. Then she softly kissed him on the forehead.

As she lifted her gaze towards Kellen Malone, the soft and troubled look of a mother's painful loss was quickly replaced by a mother's most bitter hatred.

"You killed the only person in this world who meant anything to me."

"He gave me no choice, Maggie."

"And you've given me none, Mr. Malone. This might be the last time you ever cast your eyes upon my face, but I swear before God it won't be the last time you ever feel my wrath. I'll live every day to see you in Hell."

"A couple of you men," the marshal said, "get this poor woman's son out of this dirty street."

Several of the townspeople stepped forward, stooping down to lift Jamie's body. Then they started to carry McGregor up the street to the undertaker, who'd recently began sleeping in his office, after seeing a swift upturn in business ever since Malone and Gates rode into town.

The marshal tipped his hat, before offering his hand to Maggie. "May I help you up, ma'am?"

"Thank you," she replied.

"Are you going to have this man arrested, Marshal?"

"No, ma'am, I am not."

"And why is that?"

"A couple of people have already told me that they saw your son draw first."

"But why should that matter? Malone's a gunman and extremely proficient in their use."

"Yes, I certainly know that, ma'am. But even a proficient gunman, as you call him, still has the right to defend himself." The marshal placed his hand on the woman's shoulder. "Please, ma'am, go be with your son. Make sure he's properly cared for."

Maggie nodded and started in the direction they had taken Jamie. But before she passed him, the former prostitute shot one last hateful glance at Kellen Malone.

Malone could think of nothing except to tip his hat.

As the crowd began to walk away, Gates walked over to where he was standing beside them. "You think she really meant that, Kell?"

"I have no doubt the woman means it." Then Malone remembered the sound of gunshots he'd heard earlier. "Damon, what happened back there?"

"That's the same thing I need to hear," the marshal said, interrupting their conversation. "Why don't the three of us have a chat back at the saloon, so I can get the details for my report?"

Malone stuck out his hand "How are you, Jim?" "Better than you, Malone," Cowdery said. "Maybe it's just me, but has it ever occurred to you that trouble always looks to share your saddle?"

＊ ＊ ＊ ＊

BACK AT THE MCGREGOR RANCH, THE TWO OF them lay back on their pillows, staring up at the ceiling. The man rolled over to the nightstand and began rolling himself a smoke.

Upon completing the building of his smoke, the woman had a lit match waiting for him. She lifted the flame to light the end of the cigarette between his lips.

"I understand that you and Joe Larsen were good friends," she said. "Is that true?"

"Big Joe and me were riding partners for over ten years,"

Nate Fitzsimmons said. "Reckon you could say that made us mighty close."

"Then we both lost somebody we cared about tonight."

"Why do you ask, Maggie?"

"Because somebody has to pay for their murder."

"What have you got in mind?"

"I understand Malone will be returning to Nicodemus with Mr. Gates."

"You mean the buck?"

"I don't much care for that kind of talk."

"Sorry, Maggie."

"I've already paid a couple of men to ride on ahead and wait for Mr. Malone, she said, throwing down the remainder of the whiskey glass in one gulp. "I want you to get some men together, in case they should fail, and go to Nicodemus to kill him. I am willing to pay whatever it costs."

"What about the slave?"

"I don't care about Mr. Gates. Whatever happens to him, that's between the two of you. The only thing I care about is making sure Kellen Malone is dead. Is that something you think you could do?"

"If the money's right, and after what the two of us done here, I'd even shoot my own pappy." Fitzsimmons stubbed out his cigarette, rolled over towards the woman, and placed his hand on her bare shoulder. "I reckon it will wait until the morning."

Maggie pulled away from him, rising to pull on her robe.

"No, it won't, Mr. Fitzsimmons. You will get busy with the preparations tonight. And if you fail in the attempt, it would be wise for you to keep riding."

"But what about us, Maggie?"

"There is no *us*, Mr. Fitzsimmons. There is only me." She removed a revolver from the drawer of her dresser, eared back the hammer, and pointed the barrel at the man in her bed. "Now, Mr. Fitzsimmons, you will get up, get dressed, and go and get your people together.

"If you need anything further from me, regarding money or supplies, you can come and knock at my front door. If you need anything more than that, you can find that elsewhere. Is that clear?"

Nate rose from the bed and quickly pulled on his clothes.

"You're a hard woman, Maggie McGregor."

"It's a hard life, Mr. Fitzsimmons."

CHAPTER SEVENTEEN

Sitting alone at a table in the back of the noisy and crowded saloon was a tall, lean, and quiet stranger.

Silently, the man nursed a cold beer.

The stranger listened to no one, but he heard everything around him. His green, piercing eyes darted from one customer to another. He made note of every face, quickly dismissing those who posed him no harm.

He took special note of the men who looked like they fancied themselves to be good with a gun. To those ones, he devoted a little more of his scant interest.

Sitting with his back to the wall, the man instinctively shifted his left side away from those in the saloon.

This was a habit ingrained upon him by the years. It allowed Joe to keep his gun between him and any source of impending danger. It also concealed the skull-shaped scar on his left cheek, the one that earned him the nickname of "Skull."

On this day, a conversation taking place at the next table soon caught Joe Clements' attention.

"I'm telling you, Reed, that Kellen Malone won't know

what hit him," Jace Jenkins said, pouring himself a shot of whiskey.

The other man at the table drained the last swallow of his beer. "But I've heard the man is pure-poison with a six-shooter."

"It don't really matter how good he is," Jace said. His dark eyes beamed at the idea of taking down one of the West's most legendary gunman. "There's only one of him and two of us."

"But what about the big black boy who's riding with Malone?" Reed said.

"If we have to, then we'll kill him too. Besides, ain't nobody going to miss another one of them darkies," he said, pouring another drink of whiskey from the bottle. He gulped down the liquor before continuing. "Maggie just wants Malone dead. She don't care about who else gets killed in the process."

"So, how're we going to do this, Jace?"

"Malone should be riding in here by this time tomorrow. About ten minutes later, we'll both be a couple of wealthy men."

"Ten thousand dollars for just one hombre," Reed said. "She must really be nursing a grudge against this one."

"Why not? Malone killed her son."

"You mean Maggie was Jason McGregor's ma? The whore?"

"You didn't know that?"

"I had no idea," Reed said.

Jace started to pour himself another drink, but stopped when Reed slammed his hand down over the top of his glass.

"What's that for?" Jace said.

"Just protecting my interests," Reed replied. "If we plan on collecting that money, then we need to keep our wits about us."

Jace reached over and hammered the cork back into the bottle. "Okay! Okay, Reed. It'll wait until tomorrow then."

Satisfied he'd heard everything he needed to know, Clements tossed down the last of his beer and pushed back from the table. Feigning an itch to his left cheek, Joe rubbed at it as he passed their table.

When he finally removed his hand, another man in the saloon noticed the scar and pointed it out to his drinking partner. Then he repeatedly whispered the stranger's name to the others sitting around them.

Suddenly, the crowd began buzzing about the identity of the man who was just sitting among them.

Clements continued walking like he saw none of it. The slightest trace of a smile could be seen on his lips as he pushed though the batwing doors.

* * * *

WELL AFTER THE BLACKNESS OF NIGHT ENVELOPED the town, a pair of men left the saloon, headed for the hotel. The two were laughing and swapping jokes, confident that great wealth would soon be in their future.

As they walked down the boardwalk in front of the shops and buildings, they saw a man leaned back on a bench outside the general store, his head resting against the wall. The stranger's hat was pulled down low over his face, like he was sleeping off a drunk.

Jenkins thought about kicking the man's feet out of the way, but he quickly reconsidered. This close to the arrival of their target, Jace could see no reason to draw any undue attention to themselves.

Jenkins and Reed deliberately stepped around the man's outstretched legs, before resuming their path to the hotel.

Once they passed him, the apparently-sleeping drunk pushed back his hat. Silently, he rose from his place on the bench.

"Where are you gentlemen headed?" Clements said.

Jenkins and Reed were startled by the sound of the man's voice, speaking so closely behind them.

"Not that it's any of your neverminds, friend," Jenkins said, "but we're going back to the hotel."

"No, you're not."

"We're not?" Reed said, smiling without humor. "What do you figure is going to keep us from going there?"

"I am."

"You think a mite highly of yourself, don't you, stranger?" Jenkins replied.

"Yea," Reed said, "who do you think you are?

"I'm Joe Clements."

"Are you the one they call Skull?"

Both of the men were familiar with the name. Whenever the speed of various gunfighters was discussed, Joe Clements' name was always one of the first ones mentioned. It was said that the mark on Clements cheek was the result of a knife fight.

"Some people call me that."

"Good for you," Jenkins replied. "But we'll be on our way

now."

"No, you won't."

"And why is that?" Reed said.

Joe's green eyes blazed in the darkness. "Because I plan to kill you, the both of you."

"I know all about you, mister," Jenkins said. "But we don't have any quarrel with you."

"You're wrong, friend. You have a big quarrel with me."

"What kind of fight could we have with you?" Reed asked. "We never even laid eyes on you before today."

"Are you figuring to kill Kellen Malone?"

Jenkins was suspicious. "Where'd you hear that?"

Clements simply smiled. "Inside the saloon, from you two idiots. When you're conspiring to kill someone, you might want to be more careful about who's listening to your plans."

"You still didn't answer the question," Reed said. "What kind of quarrel could we possibly have with you, stranger?"

"Malone," he replied. "He's my friend. If you have a quarrel with Malone, then your quarrel's definitely with me."

"And you figure to kill the two of us for that?"

"Yep," Clements said, pulling the makings from his shirt pocket. "But first I need me a smoke. You mind?"

Reed and Jenkins couldn't believe that Skull Clements, one of the West's most notorious gunmen, who was threatening to kill the pair of them, would stop in the middle of the conversation to make himself a cigarette.

Clements prepared his cigarette, pulling tight the bag's string with his teeth. After returning it to his pocket, he lightly licked the edge of the paper. Then he stuck the final product between his lips.

"Either of you boys got a light?"

Joe's green eyes moved from one to the other, seeing Reed's hand inching closer to his gun. "If I was you, I might rethink what you're thinking, friend."

"If you're going to kill us anyway, then why does it matter?"

"It won't matter to you. It might matter to him." Clements stared Jenkins in the eyes, while fumbling around in his pockets. "Man shouldn't be in a hurry to go to his final reward. Or in your case, the pits below. Ah, there it is. I knew I had a match here somewhere."

The two of them stood there looking at Clements in stunned disbelief. Joe simply smiled, struck his match on the side of the building, and lifted the flame to his cigarette. He took a long pull from his smoke, exhaling a nearly perfect smoke circle.

"Now, where were we?" he said. "Oh, that's right. I'm here to kill you."

Jenkins spat a fresh stream of tobacco juice on the toe of Clements' left boot. "What makes you so certain you can kill the both of us?"

"Experience," he replied, glancing down at his boot with a look of disdain. "Unlike Mr. Kellen Malone, I'm a man unshackled by the bonds of conscience. Malone might kill you, if given a good reason. But I don't need one.

"But today I have a reason. I have two. You plan on killing my friend, Malone. And then there's the boot."

"But you don't even know our names," Reed said.

"I don't need to. It's not like you're going to be around

long enough for us to grow friendly."

"Even if you do kill us," Reed said, "it won't do nothing to save your friend. Maggie McGregor already has people coming to Nicodemus to kill Malone."

"Shut up, you fool," Jenkins said.

"If we fail, it's certain they won't."

"I mean it, Reed. Shut your mouth!"

The two McGregor hands were growing tense and angry. Clements was emotionless. Their throats were dry and tight. Clements was growing increasingly bored with their conversation.

"The way I see it," Joe said, "you only have a couple of options. And only one of those options doesn't end up with the two of you dead."

"And what is that?" Reed said.

"The two of you can forget about Malone, drop your gun belts, fork your horses, and ride on out of here."

"And if we don't?"

"I've already told you that one."

"I think we'll just stay," Jenkins said, "and collect the money for Malone's hide." Jenkins spat tobacco on Clements' other boot toe. "After we're done killing you, that is."

Jace Jenkins' hand flashed for his six-gun.

Jace's gun had barely cleared the leather of his holster before a couple of Joe's slugs pierced his shirtfront. They tore an ugly path into his heart, before the McGregor ranch hand pitched forward on his face, his gun clattering onto the wooden floor.

Reed scarcely touched the butt of his hogleg before Clements' gun ended all of his tomorrows. He staggered on his feet as he saw the gun smoking in Joe's hand.

"Reckon you're as fast as they said," Reeds struggled to say, catching hold of the railing in front of the store. Then he slumped onto the floor.

Joe simply holstered his gun, took another puff of his cigarette, and wiped the toe of his boots on the unbloodied portion of Jenkins' shirt sleeve. Satisfied with the results, Clements sauntered towards the hotel, which he was certain now had a vacancy.

Along with the sounds coming from inside the saloon, the only things you could hear in the night were the foot falls of a man walking on weathered lumber and the ring of Joe's spurs as he moved.

CHAPTER EIGHTEEN

KELLEN MALONE AND DAMON GATES RODE INTO town the next morning. They weren't in town too long before they learned about the shooting of Jenkins and Reed that took place the night before.

Although nobody saw the shooting take place, it was speculated that the deed had been committed by Skull Clements, who was spotted in the saloon a couple of hours before the shooting occurred.

Further proof was given to those rumors by the fact that their room in the hotel was now occupied by Clements, who was also the one to inform the hotel manager about the sudden vacancy.

After being turned away at one of the saloons in town, Malone and Gates located another one that had no qualms about serving a black man.

As they dined on a couple big plates of beef and spuds, the smiling face of Joe Clements entered the place. He pulled up a chair next to the two men.

"How are you doing, Joe?" Malone said, before making

his introductions of all those sitting at the table.

"How's married life treating you, Joe?"

For the first time since Malone knew Clements, he thought he might have seen the first hint of a blush.

"Just fine, Kell."

"Rachel and I haven't seen much of you since you tied the knot. And how's that sweet Jenny doing?"

"She's better than fine."

"Then give her a kiss from me the next time you see her."

"I plan on giving her several, and not a one of them will be from you," Joe said, with a smile. Then he motioned at the bartender to bring him a beer. "And from what I hear about you, Kell, it sounds like you're up to your usual tricks, out winning friends."

"I heard pretty much the same thing about you, Joe. Folks hereabouts are saying you shot a couple of men last night."

"I heard that one too," Joe said. "Did you know a couple of guys named Jenkins and Reed?"

"No," Malone said. "Should I?"

"They knew you." The bartender brought him a beer and Joe stopped to taste it. "They were being paid to kill you."

"How'd you hear that?"

"From them. Somebody named Maggie hired them."

"Maggie McGregor?" Damon said.

"That's the name they used. You know her?"

"Malone killed her son."

Joe nodded while lifting his beer. "That often tends to put women in a bad frame of mind."

"But Maggie's son was trying to kill her at the time," Malone added.

175

"How is it you always find a way to make everything so complicated?"

"It's a gift."

For the next half hour, Joe listened silently while Malone explained everything that happened since he first laid eyes on Damon Gates.

"All of this just goes to prove what I've always told you," Joe said. "It's bad luck, Kell, to stop a hanging. No offense, Damon."

"None taken, Mr. Clements."

"Please call me Joe."

"Okay, Joe. But I guess you'd have to say that Malone wasn't really the one who stopped the hanging. That was Gabriel Burns."

"And look how that turned out for him," Joe replied. "But I do think your friend has a point, Kell. I reckon it could be said that you weren't really the one to break up the hanging. See! We found you a loophole."

"Thanks, Joe."

"I live to serve," Clements said. "But before we go deciding that your luck seems to be improving, Kell, you need to know something else."

"What's that?"

"You're going to have company when you get back to Nicodemus."

"What do you mean?"

"One of the men from last night," Joe explained, "said something about Maggie sending some of her hands to Nicodemus to kill you there, in case they failed."

"Nicodemus?" Damon said.

"Yep."

Malone simply laughed and took another drink of coffee. "You have any more good news for us, Joe?"

"No, that's just about it," Joe said, "except for the fact I'm coming with you."

"You're coming with us? So much for thinking my bad luck is just about over."

A look of fear came to Damon's eyes. "My Lizzie's in Nicodemus. Everyone I love is back there," he said. "I need to get back home."

"Gather up your gear, Joe, and meet us back here in about ten minutes," Malone said. "And you, Damon, better finish up your food. It might be a long ride before we get any more."

* * * *

STANDING ON THE FRONT STEP OF THE RANCH house, Maggie McGregor watched the men saddling their horses, loading their gear, and getting ready to start off for Nicodemus.

Maggie knew it would probably be the last time she would ever see such a sight on the McGregor ranch, since she had a buyer coming to see the place the following day. And the figure she'd already discussed with Thaddeus Gill was both a fair and discounted price.

With the death of her son, Maggie no longer had any reason to stay in this part of the country. She would return to Virginia, to the home of her aging parents, to a place that knew nothing of the shameful life she lived in the West.

Despite the wealth she now controlled, Maggie realized she would never be seen as anything more than the town prostitute at the occasional social gatherings, the subject of whispered gossip and insincere smiles from the women.

And the men? A number of them would always look at Maggie as an easy mark, someone to be used and exploited to satisfy their evil needs. The ones who already had her would never get over looking at the woman as they always knew her, their minds and imaginations returning to the place of their debauchery.

The only part of the West that she would continue to embrace was her bitter and dreadful hatred for Kellen Malone. And, perhaps, if the men Maggie employed were successful in their mission, she could leave that behind as well.

As Maggie watched the nearly twenty men prepare for their journey, she saw Nate Fitzsimmons come riding in her direction.

As he approached the house, Fitzsimmons examined every inch of the woman he'd often used on Saturday nights after being paid his week's wages. His was exactly the kind of look that was driving Maggie to leave the territory.

Nate drew rein in front of the woman, leaning upon his saddle horn, his eyes once more sweeping across her form from head to toe. "We're just about ready to go, Maggie. Or would you rather I call you Mrs. McGregor?"

"Maggie is fine, for now."

"Good."

"Do your men have everything you need?"

"Provisions for the trip, bedrolls, and horses, I don't know what more we'd need other than guns and ammo."

"Do you have them? Guns and ammunition, I mean?"

"Yes, Maggie. More than enough to finish the job."

"Then see that you do."

"Have you heard anything else from Jenkins and Reed?"

"Not a word," Maggie said. "I'm confident that Mr. Malone couldn't be more than a day's ride away from Nicodemus. Therefore, I would have to assume the two of them have failed in their mission."

"Then you can count on me and the boys to get him for you."

"Be sure and tell your men that Mr. Gill wants to retain their services, should we reach a final agreement on purchasing the ranch. Although I will no longer be here, those who survive will still have a place of employment."

"And what about you, Maggie?" he said, climbing down from his horse. "Where will you go?"

"Not that it's any of your business, but I shall return to Virginia."

"Come live with me, Maggie," he said, dropping the reins to the ground.

Maggie simply laughed.

"I'm serious. If you want to go to Virginia, I'll take you. Just you and me, Maggie, together as man and wife," he said, taking the former prostitute in his arms and kissing her fully on the lips.

Maggie never responded, simply waiting until Fitzsimmons pulled away from her. Then she threw back her head and laughed, a cruel and humorless response to the man's sincere words and actions. Following the laughter, her face turned as hard as marble. Then she wiped her palm across her lips, as if to wipe away any remnants of the kiss.

"And what would ever possess you to think I wanted any

of that from you?"

"But, Maggie, I thought we shared something, the two of us."

"We shared a bed, Nate. On Saturday nights, I shared my favors with you. Nothing more!"

Despite the fact that, to all those around him Nate was ruthless and cruel, the feelings he had for this woman were genuine. "But don't you want love, Maggie?"

"Love!" she said, walking over to gently run her hand along the face of Nate's horse, which nuzzled back at her in return. "Love is only a word conjured up by the authors of children's fairy tales. And love is only something believed in by silly, little school girls, who've yet to learn that it's all one big lie."

"It doesn't have to be that way," he said, placing his hand on her shoulder. "It doesn't have to be that way with me."

Maggie shook off his hand and pulled away from him.

"Wait for me, Maggie. Wait for me to come back. Then we can go wherever you want. You and me, we can go there together. Trust me! I won't treat you like Robert did. And I won't treat you like Jamie."

Whatever softness once resided in the woman's eyes was now gone in an instant. She cast a look of contempt in Fitzsimmons' direction that could only be exceeded by her loathing hatred of Kellen Malone.

"Don't you ever mention my son's name like that to me again! Do you hear me?"

"Yes, Maggie."

"Now you have a job to do, Mr. Fitzsimmons. If you succeed in killing Malone, there will be a bank draft waiting for you here, immediately upon your return. You can go now."

"But what about us?"

"You are never to speak to me again after today, Nate. And if you ever place your hand upon me from this day forward, I will hunt you down and disembowel you while you sleep. Is that clear?"

Fitzsimmons couldn't believe the sudden transformation he just witnessed in the woman before him. He backed away from her, almost missing the stirrup as he climbed on top his horse.

Nate started to speak once again, but decided against it. Still unsure of what he said or what just happened between them, he reined his horse around and started down towards the stable to meet the other riders.

Casting one final look over his shoulder, Fitzsimmons saw the woman he still loved had already gone back into the house.

* * * *

WHILE DAMON WAS WOLFING DOWN HIS FOOD AND they were waiting on Joe to return from the hotel, Malone reached into his vest pocket and removed a gold watch, a precious gift from his wife. Opening the watch, he stared at the picture of Rachel contained inside.

There was a time in his life when Malone didn't much care what happened to him. None of it really mattered to the man.

But now, Malone had a family that depended on him. No longer could he walk into a gun battle without thinking of the woman he married. Increasingly, he regretted the time he spent away from home.

It's much easier for a man to prevail in a gunfight when the outcome really doesn't matter to him.

Now, the outcome mattered to Malone.

And now that Clements was married to Jenny, it was a realization that was just dawning on him as well.

Had he not given his word to Damon's son that he would try to bring the boy's father home safely, Malone would have forked his horse and set it on a fast gallop down the trail to Redhawk.

Gates looked up from the few final bites on his plate just long enough to see his friend staring at the watch.

"Calm down, Kell," he said. "Joe hasn't even been gone ten minutes yet. We've still got time."

Malone just smiled, flipped the watch shut, and returned it to his pocket. "You still got that money that Kane and Annibel Coleman paid you?"

"Except for the price of the gun you bought me and the dress for Lizzie," he replied. Then Damon laughed. "You've been with me the whole time. Where else would I have spent it?"

"Do you trust me, Damon?"

"Sure, I do, Kell. I'd be a darned fool not to."

"Then, give me what you have left of the money."

Damon reached into his pocket, located the money, and handed the bills over to his friend. "Should I ask why?"

"Thanks, Damon. There's not time to tell you all about it now," he said. "I have to go send a telegram. If Joe gets back before I do, tell him to wait for me here. This shouldn't take too long."

182

"Okay, Kell" he said, smiling with a look of bewilderment. Then he softly muttered to himself, "Reckon I'll never understand white folks."

Malone slammed his hat back on and rushed out of the saloon, heading down the street towards the telegraph office.

Malone threw open the door, walked up to the counter, and said, "You have a pencil and a piece of paper?"

The grizzled telegraph operator, bored with the entire world, set down the apple he was eating and handed the items across the counter to Malone.

Before starting, Malone touched the end of the well-used, yellow pencil to his tongue and began scrawling out a short message on the piece of paper. Then he returned the pencil and the piece of paper to the operator.

"The man's name and town are written on top of the paper," Malone said.

The telegraph operator, still not hiding his indifference and longing to return to his apple, began reading the message in preparation for its transmission. Suddenly, his eyes grew large and excited. "Are you sure about this?" he said.

"Every word," Malone replied. "And I need it to go out immediately."

"Okay," he said, suddenly forgetting about his tasty apple.

Malone slapped eight bits down on the counter. "Will this pay for it?"

"That'll more than pay for it."

"Good." Malone said. "The rest of it's for your discretion. Do you understand?"

The man nodded as he quickly started to key the message, remembering that he specifically took this job for rare moments such as these, when his profession made him the first person in town to know about the advent of big news. The telegraph operator could hardly wait to tell his wife of forty-nine years about his day.

Closing the door behind him, Malone reopened the watch from his pocket and glanced again at the photo of his lovely Rachel.

Suddenly confident that the plans he'd just put into motion might increase the odds of seeing her again, a smile came to his face.

Malone was still smiling when he started back down the street to the saloon.

CHAPTER NINETEEN

Following the Civil War and a slain president's Emancipation Proclamation, blacks were no longer shackled by chains of iron.

Instead, their bonds were forged of poverty, illiteracy, and racial traditions, obstacles which often forced these former slaves to return to sharecropping the plantations of their former masters.

And like the Hebrew Children of Israel, laboring under the bondage of their Egyptian taskmasters, blacks were looking for another "Moses," someone to lead them to their own "Promised Land."

Handbills calling "All Colored People" to "Go to Kansas" were distributed all over the states of Tennessee and Kentucky, from which most of former slaves came.

These fliers were circulated everywhere by Benjamin "Pap" Singleton, a black Nashville carpenter, the self-proclaimed "Moses of the Colored Exodus."

Lured by the exaggerated promises of cheap and available land, wild horses which were free to be captured and broken, and the possibilities of finally governing themselves, these former slaves came to Kansas during the dark days of Reconstruction.

In the minds of Black Americans, the state of Kansas came into the Union as a Free State, purchased with the currency of blood. Seen as a place of the Underground Railroad and the home to John Brown, a firebrand of the abolitionist movement, Kansas *was* the Promised Land they sought, a destination out of the wilderness and a place friendly to their cause.

And those brave and hardy souls who made the long and difficult journey to Nicodemus soon became known as "Exodusters."

In the midst of this treeless expanse of wide, blue skies and wind-blown prairie grass of the Great Plains, next to the Solomon River, there rose up a welcomed sanctuary for the oppressed Freedmen of the South.

With the shortage of trees for lumber on the Great Plains, many of the settlers' first homes were simply dugouts, a situation which caused one of the appalled newcomers to remark that the residents of Nicodemus lived in the ground "like prairie dogs."

Later homes were mostly sod structures, finally giving way to wood when it was cheap and available. Some of the buildings in Nicodemus were constructed of magnesian limestone, taken from a quarry not too far from the town.

Thanks to these black pioneers' great vision and dogged will to survive, a thriving all-black community rose up in the heart of the country. That place was Nicodemus, an idea first conceived in the mind of W.R. Hill, a white man.

* * * *

On this day, nearly all of the two hundred residents of the town of Nicodemus were crammed into the Nicodemus First Baptist Church.

Squeezing themselves into the crowded church pews and with people standing all along the sides and back of the church house, the people of the town came out to learn about the coming threat to their once-peaceful community.

Sitting in the front row of the church, next to the family of Damon Gates, were Kellen Malone and Joe Clements.

A confirmed sinner, Clements, who hadn't been inside a church since the marriage to his wife, was firmly convinced the roof of the church might just fall upon his head before he had the chance to flee.

Once Rev. Silas Lee was satisfied that everyone had arrived, he stood up before the gathering. The reverend's shoulders were slumped and a look of great worry was on his face as he trudged to the pulpit. He stood there silently for a time, scanning many of the faces in the crowd, such as Zack and Jenny Fletcher, who were some of the town's first settlers.

"As the leader of God's precious sheep," Rev. Lee said, "I cannot presume to tell you what to do. But I do think each and every one of you has the right to voice your opinion before this matter comes to you for a vote. Now, does anyone care to make a statement? Now is your chance."

"If these men are coming here to kill this Kellen Malone, how does that make it our problem?" one of them said.

"I'm here in Kansas right now because of white men's cruelty," someone shouted above the crowd. "Why should I risk my life to help one of them?"

One of the men, a tall, strong, and rangy specimen of youth stood to his feet. "My daddy took up arms for this country, to try and win our freedom. At Antietam, he stumbled over what was left of many of his good, white brothers who died for our cause.

"Daddy served with this Kellen Malone. He fought beside him. Daddy told me about how Mr. Malone once saved his life. If we'uns won't fight side-by-side for this good and decent man, then we ain't worth the freedom so many died to win for us."

"That's crazy talk," a man shouted, earning him a look of scorn from the young son of the Civil War veteran.

A couple of people in the crowd stood to their feet with a look of disgust, before the two of them stomped out of the building. Later, as the debate continued, those who left were joined by another half dozen who angrily exited the church.

"Whites killed my husband, both of my brothers, and one of my sons," an aged black woman said. "I came here to Nicodemus to get away from the threats of fear and violence. Now, one of them is going to bring it down upon us again. Lord help us! When will we ever be free?"

"Nicodemus is our Promised Land, just like the Hebrew children had," said a generally quiet man in the back of the church. "Now, I remember the parson reading in the pages of God's book that even the Children of Israel had to fight off the giants to win their land of milk and honey. If it was good enough for the people of God, then it's right for us too!"

"I think this Malone needs to ride out now," one man said. "With him gone, maybe them men will leave us alone."

The various comments coming from the crowd were met

with occasional bursts of applause and shouts of agreement. There were also sneers and voices of disdain coming from the midst of the congregation.

A couple of men on the right side of the building nearly came to blows over some of the comments, the situation requiring a couple of people to step in between them to prevent any further controversy.

An old man, nervously twisting his hat in his hands, finally rose to speak. "My granddaddy came over to this land on a ship from Africa. He was stolen from his peoples, from his family, and from the places he knowed. But we's here now. This is our land. This be our home. And I cain't speak for no one else, but I don't plans to give up my land without a fight. There! I done gone and said what I thinks."

After letting most everybody in the room have sufficient time to make their voice heard, then Lee called upon Damon Gates to say a few words.

Damon let loose of Lizzie's comforting hand and arose from his seat. She softly patted him on the arm for strength, before he climbed the stairs to a place behind the pulpit. Gates looked out over the crowd, smiling at those faces he knew to be friendly towards him. The others, he tried to ignore.

"I want you all to know that these men who want to kill us are coming here because of me, not because of Kellen Malone. Men like these ones tried to hang me. They tried to hang me for no other reason than the color of my skin.

"But thanks to a couple of white men, a pair of gunmen, Gabriel Burns and Kellen Malone, I'm still here," Damon said, removing a handkerchief from his pocket to wipe the nervous sweat from his face. "Because of them, I'm alive to be speaking to you now. Mr. Malone wouldn't even be involved in this mess if he hadn't saved my life and then agreed to my pleas for his help.

"What you don't know and what Mr. Malone probably won't tell you is that I begged him to go with me to help some white folks in Colorado. These people weren't much different than us. They were just a bunch of poor farmers, fearful and alone. Some rich and powerful people meant to do them harm too.

"But this dirt-poor farmer didn't want my help because I was black. Then he almost let his family die before he gave up the stubborn fist-hold he had on his own hate. Mr. Malone made that happen. With his strong fist and his powerful words, Mr. Malone made this man see that we aren't that different inside.

"Black and white, no matter what our skin color, we're all people who love our families, value our land, and we treasure, above all else, the freedom God gave to us. And when we die, it's red blood that flows from all of our veins."

For a time, Damon stood silent in front of the crowd, searching for strength, looking for the proper words to persuade a fearful people to risk their lives for the life of another, someone of a different color.

"Now, I'm not just asking you to fight for Mr. Malone, I'm asking something more, much more. I'm asking you to follow him, to let Mr. Malone be our Joshua, leading us into battle with the Philistines."

A man about halfway back the aisles jumped up and said, "It's not bad enough you wants us to risk our necks for this white man, now you wants him to give us orders too, like our Massa back in Tennessee?"

"Yes," Damon said, "that's what I'm asking you to do. Mr. Malone's skin might look to be white, but his mother was a full-blooded Cherokee. Mr. Malone is a man of peace, but I've noticed when the man fights, he fights like the cursed demons of hell," Damon said, fearful that his use of the word might have offended the preacher. "No offense, Reverend."

Lee simply smiled and shook his head.

"Come to think of it," Damon continued, "Kellen Malone fights like he's one of us. Do you know why? I'll tell you. Like all of us, Mr. Malone spent several years of his life in chains, locked up for a crime he didn't commit. He knows what it is to have his freedom taken from him.

"Over the past couple of weeks, the man has become my friend. I trust him to lead us into battle. I'm asking you to do the same. Because nobody fights harder for freedom than the person who's seen it taken away from him."

Gates finished speaking, lowered his head, and ambled slowly down from the platform. He was shocked to be greeted with a smattering of applause which soon developed into a standing ovation.

Once back at his pew, Lizzie stood to embrace him and kiss him softly on the cheek. Malone and Clements stood to shake Damon's hand.

The pastor, who was then standing behind the pulpit, asked Malone if he wished to say something.

With a look of hesitation, Malone finally nodded and walked to the front of the church. Refusing to take a place behind the pulpit, he chose to stand in front of the crowd, on their level, pacing from side-to-side as he began speaking.

"It's true these men are coming to kill me," Malone said. "But as much as I'd like to tell you that forking a horse and riding down the road would stop the coming bloodshed, it simply wouldn't be true. These men are being paid by a hurt and evil woman, who's lost all sense of reason. The need to kill and the desire to make someone else pay for her suffering is all this bitter woman has left.

"If I simply ride away, the men who are coming here aren't much different than her. If I'm not here, they'll think you're only hiding my whereabouts. Then they will simply set fire to the town and harm your women and children, just like they tried to do with those squatters in Colorado.

"We have a couple of things going for us," Kell continued. "They don't think we know about their attack, so the element of surprise is on our side. If you choose to fight, then the odds are good that you'll prevail. But if you do nothing, then a great number of you men will die. And your wives and daughters might suffer a worse fate.

"The decision is yours to make. Joe and I are going to fight these men whether or not you choose to join us. But if you decide to sign on, then your best chance of victory will depend on you following my orders."

Malone stopped pacing in front of the crowd and paused to look a number of them directly in the eye. "Ladies and gentlemen, I can't tell you how to vote, but I do have something to tell you," he continued. "You are free men and women now."

"Freedom doesn't come cheap. It has to be purchased. Sacrifice, courage, and responsibility are often the price of liberty. Now is the time to choose. You must decide if your freedom is worth the cost. I've also learned that a freedom worth having is always a freedom worth defending."

Malone said nothing further as he returned to his seat. Once there, Clements simply looked him in the eye and nodded.

The pastor rose from his chair and walked over behind the pulpit. He paused to stare out over the crowd. "The time for talk is over," he said. "Now we should vote. All those men in favor of fighting with Mr. Malone, please raise your hands."

Damon's hand was the first one to be lifted, immediately followed by the Pastor. They were joined by a small handful of others. And then the number grew, until nearly every man in the building raised a hand.

"Well, Mr. Malone," the preacher said, "it looks like the matter is settled. Nicodemus is with you. What is it you need us to do?"

Just about that time, the sound of a wagon approaching could be heard outside the church. Fearing it might be the arrival of the outlaws, one of the members cracked the door to spy outside. Upon them seeing it was no threat, a number of the church people left their places to see who was coming.

Driving the wagon was a face known only to a handful of those in the room. It was Denny Abrams, the white shopkeeper from Paradise Flats. The contents of his wagon were covered with a blanket. He pulled the team of horses to a stop right in front of the church and smiled when he saw Malone push his way through the crowd.

Joe Clements and Damon Gates were only a few steps behind him.

"It's good to see you, Kell," the man said.

"Not nearly as good as it is seeing you," Malone replied, walking over to shake Denny's hand. "I was starting to fear you wouldn't make it, Denny. I'm just surprised to see you'd be the one delivering them."

"It's too big an order to trust to anyone else," Denny replied. Then he smiled "And I just couldn't resist seeing the looks on people's faces when they're finally unveiled. That, alone, will make it worth the trip."

Malone moved to the rear of the wagon and jerked away the blanket, uncovering the mysterious contents.

When the blanket was pulled away, it revealed the bed of the wagon was loaded with ammunition and forty brand new Winchester rifles. The gathering crowd began to murmur among themselves as they saw the large supply of weapons.

"Rev. Lee," Kell said, with a mile-wide grin, "this is the other reason I think we'll prevail."

The preacher smiled knowingly. "It looks like you placed a lot of faith in the eventual outcome of our vote, Mr. Malone."

"You know what the Good Book says, Reverend. 'Faith without works is dead.' I guess I just believed that good people could be persuaded to make good decisions."

"The telegram you sent back in Colby?" Damon asked. "The money you borrowed from me, Kell? Were these guns the reason?"

"It sure was."

Clements, who was standing nearby, overheard their conversation. "This is too good to pass up," he said, looking at Malone. "Go ahead and return Damon's money to him,

Kell. I'll pay Denny for the weapons. Then you can pay me back later." Joe winked at Gates. "Nothing I like better than having Malone in my debt."

As Malone watched Joe removing the bills from his wallet to pay Abrams, he handed the borrowed money back to Gates. "And thanks."

Gates hesitated as he reached for the money. "You sure?"

"It's not worth arguing with the man," Malone said. "I don't win any debates with him *or* my wife.

"What now?" Rev. Lee said.

"How many of you men know how to handle a Winchester?" Malone said, seeing only a couple of hands raised.

"Come on now, gentlemen. You're free men now," Malone added. "Nobody in Nicodemus is going to care if you know a whole lot more than you ever let on back at the plantation. Now, how many of you know how to use a Winchester?"

This time at Malone's prompting, about twenty hands went up at the question.

"That's more like it, gents. Then, all of you step forward."

Damon Gates, Denny Abrams, Rev. Lee, and Joe Clements passed out the guns and ammunition to those men, whose hands were already reaching out for them.

"That still leaves," Joe said, "about twenty more rifles, Kell."

"Make sure you hold back one of them shooters for me," Lee said.

Joe smiled and reached out to shake the man's hand. "Reverend, if we had some preachers like you and Mr. Hickman back in Redhawk, I might just start going to church more often."

"Any of you other men care to take up arms?" Damon said, as a handful of others slowly stepped forward.

"What about me?" Willina Hickman said. "I'm not a man, but if my husband, Daniel can fight for our lives, then I want to take up arms beside him."

"Why not?" Joe said, handing the woman a Winchester and a box of shells.

"The womenfolk of Nicodemus might have lived in the ground like prairie dogs," Willina said, lifting her brand new rifle skyward, "but the first sign of danger won't make us act like them."

Upon seeing one brave woman taking up arms for her town, a couple of others came forward to follow Willina's example. Always a fighter himself, Joe never once hesitated at offering any of these brave and willing souls, man or woman, a weapon.

"Joe," Malone said, "I'm going to take the experienced riflemen and assign them a place to be when the shooting starts. While I'm doing that, I want you to teach these others about the particulars of the Winchester rifle."

"Particulars?" Joe replied. "Wow! Has Miss Rachel been reading to you from Noah Webster's book again?"

"Listen, Joe, I just need you to give the reverend's flock the beginner course on how to kill the ravening wolves seeking to prey on them."

"Ravening, huh? I'm telling you, Kell, every day I rub elbows with you just makes me that much smarter. Is there anything else you need, mister general?"

"As a matter of fact, there is. As soon as you're done with

that, I want you to ride out and locate the McGregor hands. Figure out how close they are and come back here in time to give us a little warning."

"You want me to do it?" Damon said.

"No, I need you back here. Besides," Malone said, "Joe has a lot more experience with this sort of thing, getting close to people without being seen."

"Are you afraid I might get shot?" Damon asked.

"Yes, I am," Kell explained. "Joe's expendable. And if something happened out there, I'd actually miss *you*."

Malone looked over at the smiling face of his friend. "You think you can locate them for us, Joe, without getting yourself shot full of holes?"

"You'd like that, wouldn't you, Malone? Now that you owe me a little money, you're asking me to risk my neck." Joe said. "You see how he is, Damon?"

Clements put his arm around the reverend's shoulders. "All right, ladies and gentlemen, I want you to bring those shiny new rifles and follow me." Clements said. "I'll ride out and do a little recon, just as soon as I teach these good folks how to make a Winchester sing."

"I've already seen some of those McGregor hands in action, Joe. Watch your back out there."

"Sure, Malone," Clements said. "If I'm not back before nightfall, just prepare for the worst. One other thing, Kell."

"What's that?"

"You'd better pray I make it back. When it comes to a loan, Miss Jenny is meaner than a Missouri banker."

Chapter Twenty

"It's been a long, hard ride," Fitzsimmons said, speaking to his men from the saddle of his horse, "so we're going to make camp here for the night. I want you good and rested for what we have to do tomorrow.

"At first light, we're going to ride into Nicodemus under a white flag of truce. Peaceful like, we'll ask them Coloreds to hand over Malone." Nate laughed at the thought of it. "They'll probably be more than happy to hand him over to us, just to save their miserable black hides.

"But the minute we have Malone, I'll put a couple of bullets into him. That'll be your signal to attack. A town started by slaves," he scoffed. "By the time we're done, I want every one of them cotton pickers dead and the town going up in flames."

"How many of them do you figure there are?" Tom Ford said.

"I'm guessing there might be a couple hundred there, but we'll be fine," Nate explained. "We got 'em outgunned. Probably ain't more than a half dozen rifles between the bunch of 'em."

Dave Jollop, one of the riders with him turned to Fitzsimmons and said, "I came here to kill the gunman, Kellen Malone. But murdering innocent women and children, even black ones? I didn't sign on for any of this."

"You ain't just riding out of here!"

"You wanna bet?" the man said, with his rifle already trained on the ranch foreman's belly. "Me and my brother, Jess are going to ride. You do what you want here, but we won't be a party to it."

Fitzsimmons desperately wanted to kill the man for his insolence, but he knew Jollop's aim was deadly and true with that well-polished Henry.

Waving his younger brother to go on ahead, Jollop backed his horse away to cover their departure. It was only when he was well out of revolver range, that Jollop turned his back to the other riders and spurred his horse down the trail.

"Let 'em go," Nate said, spitting a green stream of tobacco juice to reinforce his point. "They're just a pair of cowards anyway. There's still eighteen of us." He looked out over his men. "Anybody else care to go?" he said. "You're free to ride away right now. But if you stay, we don't stop until every one of these Coloreds is dead. Is that clear?"

Most of the men nodded in agreement.

Ben Hopkins, a foul-smelling, hard case among the men spoke up, "But you don't care what we do with them before we kill them, do you?"

Fitzsimmons rubbed the thick stubble on his face and smiled. "Just so long as you leave one of them dark-skinned gals for me."

* * * *

LESS THAN A HUNDRED YARDS AWAY FROM THE MEN, hiding among the prairie grass, Joe Clements was watching the outlaws and determining their strength.

At this distance, Joe was confident he could kill any one of these men with a single rifle shot. He'd done it before, from much greater distances.

For a second, Clements considered shooting down their boss. And he might have done it, if Joe knew he could have gotten away clean.

If he was captured or killed, that would leave no one to tell Malone. Joe smiled to himself, realizing he feared his best friend's wrath more than the guns of these men.

Then he saw that something was happening between the outlaws.

Although he had no idea what was being said between the two men, it looked like they were having some kind of a falling out. All doubt was eliminated when Joe saw the rifle pointed at the leader's belly.

As he watched the two men ride away, Clements suddenly had an idea.

Inching his way back to where his horse was hidden, Joe mounted his horse to ride on down the trail.

For just a second, one of Nate's men thought he saw something moving in the prairie grass. But he dismissed the idea, when a second glance told him it was gone.

It was probably just a ghost of the prairie lands.

* * * *

IT WAS NIGHTFALL OVER NICODEMUS.

Malone was pacing. Clements hadn't returned.

For about the third time in the past hour, Malone checked his twin guns. The pair of them were still loaded. Standing outside Williams' general store, Malone looked up and down the street.

Lights were on inside all the stores and buildings, but nobody was on the street. In the glow coming from a couple of the windows, Malone could make out a couple of the men who he'd placed on guard duty.

As Malone was staring off into the distance, Damon's wife, Lizzie brought him a hot cup of coffee.

"Don't worry about him," she said. "Mr. Clements will be back."

"I'm not worried."

"You and Damon are so much alike."

"What do you mean, ma'am?"

"Both of you are lousy liars."

Malone smiled and tasted his coffee. "This is good. Thank you, ma'am."

"Please call me Lizzie," she replied. "And that is one more way you're both alike. Damon likes to change the subject too."

Malone laughed at the woman's comment. "And you, Lizzie, you're starting to remind me of Rachel."

"You mind if I ask you a question?"

"Sure," he said, leaning against a post as Damon's wife took a seat outside the store. "I can't make you any guarantees, Lizzie, but I'll try to give you an answer."

Lizzie sat there for a time, searching for a way to ask the question. "Why are you doing this? Why did Damon have to go help a bunch of people he never met? And why is a notorious gunman like Mr. Clements helping you?"

Malone took another drink of his coffee and cast another quick look off into the distance before answering.

"Joe isn't notorious; Joe's my friend, a friend I'm going to kill if he ain't already dead. His part in all this is easy, Lizzie. And now that Damon has become my friend too, that's why I'm here. As to the rest of it," he said, rubbing his chin, "that's a little more complicated.

"If a man's any good," Malone continued, "it's hard for him to walk away from broken things without doing something to fix them. That tells me your Damon is a good man. I don't guess I can explain it any other way than that."

"Does your wife know you think this way, Kell?"

"Yes."

"Does she understand it?"

"Rachel *accepts* it. Nothing more."

"Sounds like a good woman."

"Better than any man deserves," Malone said, "as are you, Lizzie."

Whatever else the two of them might have said was interrupted by the sound of a whistle, a warning signal from one of Malone's posted sentries. Malone drew both his guns and stared into the blackness of the night.

In the night, they could hear a single rider coming their way.

"It's Clements," the lone rider called out. "I'd just hate it

202

if you all shot me."

Clements continued on down the street, drawing rein when he saw Malone. "Reckon I'm a little late."

"Look, Lizzie! The Prodigal has returned."

"And there you are," Joe replied, "waiting for my return. Thanks, dad."

"That's okay. I sent the money I owed you to your wife Jenny. She used it to run off with a Mississippi River gambler and they're very happy together." Taking another sip of his coffee, Malone said, "After being gone this long, Joe, I hope you came back with something other than dumb excuses."

Clements cast a jealous eye at Malone's coffee. "You got any more of that?"

Lizzie jumped up from her seat. "I'll go get you one, Mr. Clements. That'll give you men a chance to talk."

"Thanks, Miss Lizzie," Clements said, climbing down from his horse and tying the reins to the post that supported the roof.

"And by the way, Kell," Lizzie said, "thanks for taking the time to chat with me."

Kell nodded. "It's my pleasure. Hope it helped."

"Maybe a little," she replied, before rushing off to prepare some more coffee.

"Glad to see you could make it, Joe," Malone said. "Damon was thinking you got yourself killed and wanted to send out a search party. Me, I was trying to organize a party to celebrate."

"I would've been back earlier," he said, plopping himself down in the chair that Lizzie just vacated, "but then I started thinking about how Kellen Malone might do it. And Miss

Rachel says you like to keep folks guessing about your where-abouts. Now, do you plan on talking until the shooting starts or do you want to know what I learned out there?"

"Let's hear it."

"We're looking at eighteen of them, headed up by some hombre by the name of Nate Fitzsimmons. They're coming at first light. One other thing, don't pay any mind to their white flag."

"And how do you know all that?"

"A couple of their boys didn't have the stomach for what Fitzsimmons had in mind for us. They had words with the man and rode away. I decided to talk to them about what this man might be planning. That's why it took me so long," he said, starting to build himself a smoke. "I had to catch up to them first. And after hearing what they told me, it's a darn good thing I did!"

"And these two men just willingly *volunteered* this information?"

"Volunteered isn't exactly the word I'd use for it," Clements said. "They needed a little bit of gentle persuasion at first, but they came around pretty fast after that."

More than once, Malone had seen Joe's methods of *gentle persuasion*. There was no further need for him to even bother asking how the information was acquired. "Did the two of them ride away happy to have done their part for the good of society?"

"The two of them rode away," Joe said, "wiser and better citizens than they were when they rode up, I might add."

"You're all heart, Joe."

CHAPTER TWENTY-ONE

O NCE MORE, MALONE ASSEMBLED THE TOWNS- people inside the doors of First Baptist Church. Reverend Lee officiated the meeting.

"This` evening, Joe Clements learned that the outlaws are planning to come in under a white flag," Malone told the crowd. "They're going to ask you to hand me over. And after you do, then they plan to kill all of you and set fire to the town.

"If it was strictly up to Joe, we'd just shoot the riders on sight. But I'm willing to give them a chance to back away or surrender.

"When they ride up," Malone said, "I plan to speak to them and give them a chance to back down. But I want you to be clear about one thing; any hostile actions on their part will be met with violence on ours. And should it come to that, you're free to choose a target and fire at will.

"You all have your assignments. You all have a job to do," Malone continued. "I'm counting on you to be in your place. Good luck to each one of you! I'm proud to stand beside you."

When Malone sat down, Rev. Lee rose to his feet and made his way up to the pulpit. He looked out over the crowd and started to speak.

"No doubt some of you are feeling a little fearful right now. I know I am. But do you remember the circulars that first told you about Nicodemus?

"I thought I should remind you of the poem that was printed on some of them. It went something like this:

> *Nicodemus was a slave of African birth*
> *And was bought for a bag of gold;*
> *He was reckoned a part of the salt of the earth;*
> *But he died years ago, very old.*
>
> *Nicodemus was a prophet; at least he was wise,*
> *For he told of the battle to come;*
> *How we trembled with fear, when he rolled up*
> *his eyes,*
> *And we heeded the shake of his thumb.*

"Nicodemus was named after a legendary African Prince, taken by force from the land of his birth and placed on one of the first slave ships bound for America. It's been said that Nicodemus later purchased his freedom. Tomorrow, we will do the same.

"In the pages of Holy Writ," Rev. Lee said, "we also read about a man named Nicodemus, who came to Jesus by night. Therefore, I think it's only fitting that we should come unto the Lord this night. Would you care to bow your heads and join me in a word of prayer?"

Following the reverend's prayer, Joe Clements lifted his

eyes and turned to Malone. "It's good they came before Jesus tonight, Kell, because it's certain they're going to face hell in the morning."

* * * *

THE SUN WAS JUST RISING OVER THE EASTERN plains when Nate Fitzsimmons and his men rode into Nicodemus. Like victorious troops returning from war, the riders fanned out across the street. And like expected, they rode in under a white flag.

Malone had prepared his troops well.

Not a single person was visible on the rooftops.

All of the men stopped when Fitzsimmons drew rein and the men formed a circle. As they looked around, their horses facing in all directions, the riders saw a number of curious and fearful faces staring at them through the windows.

"My name is Nate Fitzsimmons," the outlaw said, speaking loud enough so that the people inside might hear him. "I've come here to get Kellen Malone and his black friend, Damon Gates. No harm has to come to the rest of you, if the two of them come out here right now."

"We're right here," Malone said, stepping out of the general store and walking right down the street towards the riders. Matching him stride-for-stride, on each side of him was Joe Clements and Damon Gates.

Fitzsimmons laughed at the sight of them.

"I know both you and Gates, but who's that with you, Malone?"

"I'm Joe Clements."

At the mention of the name, Fitzsimmons eyes danced at

the idea that he and his men would be responsible for killing two of the West's fastest gunmen. He figured the death of Damon Gates would just be a bonus.

"We don't have any fuss with you today, Skull."

"Lot of folks been telling me that lately," Clements said, his green eyes turning cold underneath the brim of his hat. "I killed the last two. By the way, Fitz, I talked to Jollop and his brother. You can tell your boys to drop that white flag."

Upon hearing those words, seeing Skull Clements, and knowing he was going to need all his hands for shooting, the man holding the flag was more than happy to drop it into the dirt.

"I'll kill both of them on sight the next time we meet."

"There isn't going to be any *next time* for you," Malone said, "not unless you tell your boys to drop their guns in the dirt and ride on out of here."

"What are you talking about, Malone? You think the three of you have any chance against the bunch of us?"

"Nope, but I figure if the shooting starts, Joe and I will get at least four to six of you. And Mr. Gates, here, he's going to put a bullet through your guts. Won't you, Damon?"

"That's my plan," he replied.

"And there's one other thing you need to know," Malone said. "Ladies and gentlemen, show them!"

At the sound of Malone's order, about forty armed men and women stepped forward, exposing themselves from the rooftops and doorways. In unison, the armed black citizens of Nicodemus levered rifle shells into the chambers of their Winchesters.

The men on horseback cringed as they looked around

and above them, seeing forty, shiny new rifles pointed in their direction.

It was an ominous and unexpected sight to those riders on horseback.

"What is this, Nate? You told us there wouldn't be more than a handful of guns in this town," Ty Evans said.

"Yea," Ben Hopkins added, "it looks like they've got all the tribes in Africa here, and they done traded their spears for Winchesters."

At the sight of it, a couple of the other riders backed their horses away and spurred their horses into a gallop. The tails of their mounts were stretched out into the wind as they raced away from the town of Nicodemus forever.

When Fitzsimmons turned his eyes away from the guns and back on the three men standing in front of him, he saw that only smiles greeted him.

"It's only fair that I tell you," Malone said, "that I've instructed these good folks to open fire on you, at the first sign of any hostile intentions."

"I should've let Jamie McGregor kill you," Fitzsimmons said. "You probably didn't know that, did you? When those other riders interfered in our business, Jamie had a rifle trained on you outside the Coleman place. Wish he'd killed you now."

Bitter and angry that his plans had gone awry, Fitzsimmons had been so sure that he would have his way with the people of this town. He'd also planned to have his way with their women. Worst of all, Nate never figured on them being this well-armed.

After all, they're only a bunch of dumb slaves.

"None of that matters now," Malone said. "And the only choice you have left, Nate, is for you and your men to throw down your guns."

"That isn't my only choice," Nate said, grabbing for his gun.

Upon seeing Fitzsimmons pull iron, a trio of six-guns belched flame in his direction, with Damon's slug being the slowest one of the three.

Nate was slammed backwards over the tail of his horse, hitting the ground dead with three bullet holes in the front of his vest.

As a result of Nate's decision to draw, the other outlaws would never be given the chance to throw down their guns.

Instructed by Malone to fire at the first signs of hostile action, the people of Nicodemus immediately opened fire on the riders, working the levers and firing again and again.

The morning erupted with the sharp cracks of rifles firing, horses pitching, and the tortured cries of the dying. And the dense clouds of gun smoke that lifted from the streets of Nicodemus obscured the bright, orange light of the morning sun.

Almost sixty seconds later, when the smoke cleared around them and the guns fell silent, Kellen Malone, Joe Clements, and Damon Gates were the only ones left standing in the street.

Malone and Clements punched out the empties and reloaded their guns.

Damon stood there silent, looking down at the carnage, the streets littered with the dead and wounded, horses *and* men. Then he stared down at the gun in his hand.

The massacre was a gruesome scene for many of those involved, causing many of the citizens to become ill or to turn away their eyes from the sight of the blood-bathed streets, stains which would take a number of heavy rains to wash away.

Willina Hickman and a couple of other women moved among the fallen, seeking to aid those who were wounded. About six armed men covered the women, in case any of the wounded outlaws tried to harm them.

Only about three of the townspeople suffered injuries and nobody was killed, an outcome much better than Malone expected.

Reverend Silas Lee walked down the street, still carrying his Winchester. The man of God did his best to work up a smile.

"Glad to see you came out of this unscathed," Malone said.

"Thanks, Mr. Malone. I am pleased to see you as well."

"Looks like the Lord heard your prayer, Reverend," Joe said.

"Not this time, Mr. Clements" Lee replied. "I was praying there wouldn't be any need for bloodshed. And I did more than my share of it."

"Somewhere in that sacred Book of yours, it says, 'The way of transgressors is hard.' Am I wrong?"

"Perhaps I owe you an apology, Mr. Clements. I suppose I never figured you for a Bible reader."

"My mother was."

"Maybe there's still some hope for you then."

"Not unless the Lord starts dropping His standards."

* * * *

As Malone and Clements prepared to leave, Jacob walked over to Kell and stuck out his hand, "Thank you, Mister Kell, for taking care of my daddy."

Malone shook the boys hand and smiled. "It was my pleasure, son. Your pa's a good man. You take care of him."

While holding a sack tucked under his left arm, Damon shook Joe's hand, "It's been good to know you, Joe."

"Same here," Joe said. "Any friend of Malone's, well, any friend of Malone is someone who needs his head examined."

Damon shook Malone's hand. "Thanks for everything , Kell. There just ain't words to say..."

"I know," Malone said.

Damon handed Malone a poke. "I want you to have this."

"What is it?"

"It's my belt and gun."

"But this belongs to you, Damon. You paid me for it. Remember?"

"I know I did, Kell. But in the past few weeks, I've seen what a gun reputation does to a man. I don't want that for me. I don't want it for Lizzie."

"Are you sure?"

"Yes, Kell, I'm sure."

"Malone fished in his pocket for money. "You want me to pay you for it?"

"No," Damon said. "I trust you."

"Bad choice, Damon," Clements said. "Real bad choice."

* * * *

"MAY I TAKE YOUR HAT?" THE BUTLER SAID.

"No, I think I'll keep it," the man said. "I probably won't be here long."

"Then, please follow me, sir."

The aged, black butler led the Pinkerton detective down the hallway through the beautiful, spacious, and well-furnished Virginia mansion.

Upon seeing the extremely attractive woman, dressed in the latest styles of Paris, the detective promptly removed his hat and wondered about his appearance.

"Would you care to be seated?"

"No, thank you, ma'am. I have that information you requested."

"Yes."

The detective pulled a piece of paper from his breast pocket, unfolded it, and read from the text:

> *"Mr. Nathan Fitzsimmons was confirmed dead and seventeen of his accomplices were killed and/or imprisoned for their unprovoked attack on the town of Nicodemus, Kansas. Mr. Kellen Malone returned unharmed to his wife and home in Redhawk, in the Arizona Territory."*

The woman revealed no emotion when the paper was read.

The Pinkerton agent re-folded the piece of paper and returned it to his pocket, that time revealing the well-worn revolver that rested on his hip, concealed underneath the man's coat tail.

"Why, thank you, Detective Thomas, was it? I never imagined that the Pinkerton Agency employed agents as tall and handsome as you are," she said, rising from her chair and taking his arm.

"Have you ever considered a career in private detective work, perhaps working for yourself, Mr. Thomas?"

"No, ma'am, I haven't."

The woman took him by the arm and led him up the hall towards the dining room. "Perhaps we can discuss the matter over dinner," she said. "And please call me Maggie."

The End

Author's Note

Many Americans don't know or simply haven't been taught that black Americans played a significant role in the taming of the great American West.

In my book, you've just read about Nicodemus, Kansas, a real and once-thriving community founded by black Americans following the Civil War. Although the story is fictional, a number of the names I've used in this story were actual residents of the town.

Following the end of the Civil War until early in the next century, approximately 35,000 drovers pushed cattle from Texas to Kansas. Of these men who drove herds across prairies, through storms and swollen rivers, and journeyed through arid wastelands in order to reach the markets and railheads, it is believed that almost one-third of them were black.

Unlike much of the country, that often-falsely considered itself to be much more civilized and enlightened at the time, the American West was actually a place where a person of color could often be measured by the content of his character.

How a man went about his daily duties and met his responsibilities on a cattle drive were much more important than the color of a man's skin. Respect and equality could often be earned by the sweat of one's brow.

For some entertaining and insightful reading, I challenge you to learn more about the exploits of Jim Beckwourth, Isom Dart, Bass Reeves, Nat Love, Bill Pickett, and other black Americans of the Old West.

There is a wealth of knowledge out there waiting for others to discover.

Acknowledgements

Writing books is similar to being a pitcher in Major League Baseball. It's a solitary exercise, but you generally enjoy a much greater level of success when you have a great team behind you.

And I have certainly been blessed to be surrounded by a great team.

First of all, I am supported by a kind, attractive, and loving wife, who is both my best friend and most trusted advisor. On top of all that, she's just doggone cute to look at.

If that wasn't enough, Jo is also an outstanding photographer, her talents largely self-taught. The pictures you see of me on my book covers have all been taken by her.

Although my wife makes no pretext of understanding the mind of a writer, she fiercely believes in me and my writing. Moreover, she was the one person who primarily supported and encouraged me in the effort when it often seemed like nobody else in the publishing world ever would.

The technological challenges and difficulties that I occasionally have to confront are solved by my son, Logan, who loves and studies new technological gizmos like I follow the newest West Virginia football recruits or the latest lever-action firearm.

Logan's interest in these things and willingness to share his knowledge and expertise with me allows me to devote more of my time to writing. And Mountaineer football.

After spending time with my wife, of course.

My sister, Kathy, routinely helps me to clean up the grammatical and typing errors, which greatly tend to annoy me whenever they make it through to publication. And when they do, you can rest assured it's probably my fault, not hers.

As an author, it would be hard to find a better situation than I currently enjoy at White Feather Press. Not only is Skip Coryell my editor and publisher he's also a person I can proudly call my friend. And in my occasional conversations with other editors and agents, they routinely tell me that there are lots of authors who would gladly trade places with me.

Unfortunately for them, I have no plans on changing teams.

Finally, when it comes to matters of team, I'd like to take this time to recognize the members of the West Virginia Writers, which is a home to some of the most talented and friendly people in the country. This organization, of which I am delighted and honored to be a member, is truly a great resource for any upcoming or established author.

As a result of my membership there, I have become acquainted with a great number of writers, authors, agents, and editors, all of whom are anxious to lend you a hand or a word of encouragement, whatever the need and whenever it arises.

It's easier to pitch with a team like that behind you.

Perhaps there's one more thing that writing has in common with being on the pitcher's mound: It's a lot more fun to perform in front of a packed crowd.

Apart from matters of faith and family, perhaps the most satisfying thing in my life is knowing that others enjoy what

I write.

Therefore, I wanted to take this opportunity to thank the many dedicated readers of my books. Any author would be remiss to forget his readers; for without you, none of this would be possible.

I never get tired of meeting and talking to you. Your comments about my books are always appreciated. And the reviews you post on places like Amazon are both flattering and humbling.

I tip my hat to you.

You have my commitment that I will always do my best to keep bringing you stories that are worth the telling and books that are worth reading.

Thanks again!

— RG Yoho

Author R.G. Yoho was born in Parkersburg, West Virginia. While he was still a child, his parents moved the family to a cattle farm in southeastern Ohio.

Yoho's passion for Westerns began with the reading of *Flint*, a novel by famed Western author, Louis L'Amour.

In addition, R.G. has also published three works of non-fiction, the most recent a work of history, *America's History Is His Story*.

Married for over thirty years, R.G. is the father of three and the grandfather of two. He is also a devoted fan of West Virginia University football and basketball.

Books by RG Yoho

<u>Novels</u>
Death Comes to Redhawk
Death Rides the Rail
Long Ride to Yesterday
Nightfall Over Nicodemus

<u>Nonfiction</u>
America's History is His Story
Major Impact: The Major Harris Story